Girl Scouts in the Rockies

by

Lillian Elizabeth Roy

Double 9 BOOKS

Girl Scouts in the Rockies
by Lillian Elizabeth Roy

ISBN: 978-93-61422-83-6

Published by

DOUBLE 9 BOOKS
2/13-B, Ansari Road
Daryaganj, New Delhi – 110002
info@double9books.com
www.double9books.com
Tel. 011-40042856

ABOUT THE AUTHOR

Lillian Elizabeth Roy, an American writer born in 1868, is first-class known for her contributions to kid's literature, particularly her collection of Girl Scout novels. Among her many works, "Girl Scouts within the Rockies" stands out as a masterpiece. This book follows the adventures of a set of Girl Scouts as they embark on an interesting journey thru the majestic Rocky Mountains. Roy's writing style is characterized through its vivid descriptions and tasty storytelling, which captivate readers of every age. Through her characters, she imparts crucial values such as teamwork, braveness, and resilience, making her books no longer only unique but also educational. "Girl Scouts inside the Rockies" takes readers on a memorable expedition packed with exhilaration, challenges, and unforgettable encounters with nature. As the scouts navigate the rugged terrain and face diverse obstacles, they study valuable existence lessons that form their person and foster non-public boom. Roy's enduring legacy lies in her ability to inspire generations of readers via her undying memories of journey, friendship, and the spirit of exploration. "Girl Scouts inside the Rockies" keeps to enchant audiences nowadays, cementing Lillian Elizabeth Roy's location as a loved creator in children's literature.

CONTENTS

CHAPTER ONE
OUTFITTING FOR THE TRIP

"Girls, this is our third Summer as the Dandelion Troop of Girl Scouts,—do you realize that fact?" commented Mrs. Vernon, generally called "Verny" by the girls, or "Captain" by her friends.

"That first Summer in camp seems like mere child's play now, Verny," returned Juliet Lee, known as "Julie" or just "Jule" by her intimates.

"That really wasn't camping, at all,—what with all the cooked food our families were bringing weekly to us, and the other housekeeping equipment they brought that day in the 'furniture shower,'" Joan Allison added, giggling as she remembered the incident.

"But last Summer in the Adirondacks was real camping!" declared Ruth Bentley, nodding her head emphatically.

"Yes. Still it wasn't anything like this year's camping experience promises to be,—in the Rocky Mountains," replied Mrs. Vernon. "Mr. Gilroy furnished the tents and cots and other heavy camping things last summer, but this year we will have to do without such luxuries."

"We don't care what we have to do without, Verny, because we are so thankful to be here at all!" exclaimed Anne Bailey, who was one of the five additional scout members admitted to the circle of the four founders of Dandelion Troop the preceding summer.

"I'm so sorry the other girls can't be with us this trip," remarked Julie, who was Scout Leader of the troop.

"It's a shame that Amy's mother treats her as if she were a babe. Why, this sort of trip is exactly what the girl needs to help her get rid of her nerves," said Joan.

"Yes; didn't every one say how well she was after last summer's camp in the Adirondacks?" added Ruth Bentley.

"Poor Amy, she'll have to stay home now, and hear her mother worry about her all summer," sighed Betty Lee, Julie's sister.

"Well, I am not wasting sympathy on Amy, when dear old Hester needs all of it. The way that girl pitched in and helped earn the family bread when her father died last winter, is courageous, say I!" declared Julie.

"We all think that, Julie. And not a word of regret out of her when she found we were coming away, with Gilly, to the Rockies," added Joan.

"Dear old pal! We must be sure to write her regularly, and send her souvenirs from our different stopping-places," said Mrs. Vernon, with tears glistening in her eyes for Hester's sacrifice.

"If Julie hadn't been my sister, I'm sure Mrs. Blake would have frightened May into keeping me home," announced Betty. "When she told sister May of all the terrible things that might happen to us in the Rockies, Julie just sat and laughed aloud. Mrs. Blake was real angry at that, and said, 'Well, May, if your mother was living *she'd* never allow her dear little girls to risk their lives on such a trip.'"

Julie smiled and added, "I told Mrs. Blake, then and there, that mother would be delighted to give us the opportunity, and so would any sensible mother if she knew what such a trip meant! Mrs. Blake jumped up then, and said, I'm sure I'm as sensible as any one, but I wouldn't *think* of letting Judith and Edith take this trip.'"

"I guess it pays to be as healthy as I am," laughed Anne Bailey, who was nicknamed the "heavyweight scout," "'cause no one said I was too nervous to come, or too delicate to stand this outing."

The other scouts laughed approvingly at Anne's rosy cheeks and abundant fine health.

The foregoing conversation between Mrs. Vernon and five girl scouts took place on a train that had left Chicago, and Mr. Vernon, the day before. He had had personal business to attend to at that city, and so stopped over for a few days, promising to join the Dandelion Troop at Denver in good time to start on the Rocky Mountain trip.

"It's perfectly lovely, Verny, to think Uncle is to be one of our party this summer," remarked Joan. "He and Mr. Gilroy seem to get on so wonderfully, don't they?"

"Yes, and Mr. Gilroy's knowledge of camping in the Rockies, combined with Uncle's being with us, lightens much of the responsibility I felt for taking you all on this outing," answered Mrs. Vernon.

"It will seem ages for us to kill time about Denver when we're so anxious to get away to the mountains," said Julie.

"But there's plenty to do in that marvelous city; and lots of short trips to take that will prove very interesting," returned the Captain.

"Besides, we will have to get a number of items to add to our outfits," suggested Ruth.

"That reminds me, girls; the paper Uncle gave me as he was about to leave the train is a memo Mr. Gilroy sent, about what to take with us for this jaunt. Shall I read it to you now?" asked Mrs. Vernon.

"Oh yes, do!" chorused the girlish voices; so Mrs. Vernon opened the page which had been torn from a letter addressed to Mr. Vernon by Mr. Gilroy. Then she began reading:

"About taking baggage and outfit for this trip in the Rockies, let me give you all a bit of advice. Remember this important point when considering your wardrobe, etc.,—that we will be on the move most of the time, and so every one must learn how to do *without* things. We must travel as the guides and trappers do—very 'light.' To know when you are 'traveling light' follow this rule:

"First, make a pyramid of everything you think you must take for use during the summer, excluding the camp outfit, which my man will look out for at Denver.

"Next, inventory the items you have in the heap. Study the list earnestly and cross out anything that is not an actual necessity. Take the articles eliminated from the heap, throw them behind your back, and pile up the items that are left.

"Then, list the remainder in the new pyramid, and go over this most carefully. Cast out everything that you have the least doubt about there being an imperative need of. Toss such items behind you, and then gather the much smaller pyramid together again.

"Now, forget all your past and present needs, all that civilized life claims you should use for wear, or camp, or sleep, and remove everything from the pyramid excepting such articles as you believe you would have to have to secure a living on a desert island. If you have done this problem well, you ought to have a list on hand, after the third elimination, about as follows:

"A felt hat with brim to shed the rain and to shade your eyes from the sun; a good all-wool sweater; winter-weight woolen undergarments that will not chill you when they are dripping with water that is sweated out from within, or soaked through from without; two or three large handkerchiefs, one of silk to use for the head, neck, or other parts of the body in case of need; three pairs of heather stockings,—one pair for day use, one pair to wear at night when it is cold, and the third pair to keep for extra need; high boots—one pair to wear and one to carry; two soft silk shirts—shirt-waists for you girls; a *pure wool* army blanket; one good rubber blanket; a toothbrush, hairbrush and comb, but no other toilet articles. Be sure to have the girl-scout axe, a steel-bladed sheath knife, a *compass*, the scout pocket-knife, fishing tackle, and a *gun*. (More about this gun hereafter, girls.)

"Now, being girl scouts, you will naturally wear the approved scout uniform. If possible, have this made up in good wiry serge that will shed dust and other things, along the trail. You will want a good strong riding-habit, and two pairs of silk rubber bloomers, the latter because of their thin texture and protection against moisture.

"Wear a complete outfit, and then pack your extras in the blanket; roll the bundle in the rubber blanket, and buckle two straps about the roll. Then slip this in the duffel-bag, and you are ready.

"About the gun. Don't let your parents have a panic over the item mentioned. You girls had excellent target practice all last winter, so the fact of your carrying a rifle on this trip should not unduly excite any one. In the Rockies, a gun is as necessary as an axe or knife, and no one incurs a risk from carrying such a weapon unless he is careless. Being trained scouts, with experience back of you, you will be perfectly safe on this outing even though you do carry a rifle.

"An old Indian guide that I had some years ago, sent word that he would be happy to give us his time for the summer. So he will attend to all the camping needs,—utensils and canvas and horses, for the trip. I told him that we would have a party of girls with us this time, and he smiled when he said he would have to add needle and thread, cold cream, and such requisites to his list."

"There, girls," continued Mrs. Vernon, when she had concluded the reading of Mr. Gilroy's instructions, "that is about all Gilly said about the outfit. But I knew we had conformed to most of these requirements already, so there is nothing more to do about it. When we go over the duffel-bags in Denver, Gilly may ask you scouts to throw out your manicure cases, or whimsical little things you deem an absolute necessity now, and several articles of wear that you think you must take, but, otherwise, we are ready to 'travel light,' as he says."

"Shan't we take our sleeping-bags, Verny?" asked Ruth.

"Gilly doesn't say a word about them, so I don't know whether he forgot them, or thought you left them home."

"I wonder what sort of an outfit the guide will take?" remarked Julie.

"Aluminum-ware for cooking, and a cup, plate, and cutlery for each member of the party, Uncle Vernon said," answered Mrs. Vernon.

Just before reaching Denver, Mrs. Vernon asked of the eager scouts, "Did you girls read the books I mentioned, to become familiar with this wonderful country through which we are going to travel?"

"I read all I could, and I'm sure the other girls did, too, because every time I asked for one of those books at the Public Library I was informed it was out. Upon investigation, I learned that one or the other of Dandelion Troop was reading it," laughed Julie.

"Well, then, you learned that Colorado can boast of more than fifty mountain peaks, each three miles or more in height; a hundred or so nearly that high. And between these peaks can be found the wildest gorges, most fertile valleys and plains, that any state in the Union can boast.

"And because of these great peaks with their snow-capped summits, many of which are snowy all the year round, the flow of water from the melting snows furnishes the many scenic streams that give moisture to the plains; which in turn produce the best crops in the West.

"But the plains and valleys were not the attraction that first brought pioneers to Colorado. It was the gold and silver hidden in the mountains, and the upthrust of valuable ore from the sides of the canyons and gulches that was the magnet which caused mankind to swarm to this state. Thus, you see, it became generally populated, the mountainous, as well as the ranch sections."

While riding westward from Chicago, the gradual rise of the country failed to impress the scouts, so they were all the more surprised when Mrs. Vernon exclaimed, "I verily believe I am the first to see Pike's Peak, girls!"

"Oh, where? where?" chorused the scouts, crowding to the windows on the side of the train where the Captain sat.

"Away off there—where you see those banks of shadowy clouds! There is one cloud that stands out more distinctly than its companions—that's it," replied the Captain.

"Oh, Verny, that's not a peak!" laughed Joan.

"Of course not! That's only a darker cloud than usual," added Julie, while the other scouts laughed at their Captain's faulty eyesight.

Mrs. Vernon smiled, but kept her own counsel, and half an hour later the girls began to squint, then to doubt whether their hasty judgment had been correct, and finally to admit that their guide and teacher had been quite right! They saw the outline of a point that thrust itself above the hanging clouds which hid its sides in vapor, and the point that stood clearly defined against the sky was Pike's Peak!

"But it isn't snow-clad, and it isn't a bit beautiful!" cried Ruth in disappointment.

"Still it is the first Rocky Mountain peak we have seen," Betty Lee mildly added.

"Scouts, this is known as 'The Pike's Peak Region,'" read Julie from a guide-book.

"It ought to be called 'Pike's Bleak Region,'" grumbled Anne. "I never saw such yellow soil, with nothing but tufts of grass, dwarfed bushes, and twisted little trees growing everywhere."

Mrs. Vernon laughed. "Anne, those tufts are buffalo grass, which makes such fine grazing for cattle; and your dwarfed bushes are the famous sage-brush, while the twisted trees are cottonwoods."

"Oh, are they, really?" exclaimed Anne, now seeing these things with the same eyes but from a changed mental viewpoint.

"And notice, girls, how exhilarating the air is. Have you ever felt like this before—as if you could hike as far as the Continental Range without feeling weary?" questioned Mrs. Vernon.

When the train pulled in at Denver, Mr. Gilroy was waiting, and soon the scouts were taken to the hotel where he had engaged accommodations for the party.

"Don't say a word until you have washed away some of that alkali dust and brushed your clothes. Then we will go out to view the village," laughed he, when the girls plied him with questions.

But the scouts wasted no time needlessly over their toilets, and soon were down in the lobby again, eager for his plans.

"Now I'll tell you what Uncle wired me from Chicago to-day," began Mr. Gilroy, when all were together. "He'll be there three days longer, so we've almost five days to kill before meeting him at this hotel."

"I've engaged two good touring cars, and as soon as you approve of the plan, we will start out and see the city. To-morrow morning, early, we will motor to Colorado City and visit Hot Springs, and all the points of interest in that section. Then we can return by a different route and embrace dear old Uncle, who will be waiting for us. How about it?"

"How needless to ask!" exclaimed Mrs. Vernon, when the chorus of delight had somewhat subsided. Mr. Gilroy laughed.

"Come on, then! Bottle up the news, and stories of crime you experienced on the way West from New York, until we are *en route* to Colorado Springs. Then you can swamp me with it all," said he.

So that day they visited the city of Denver, which gave the scouts much to see and talk about, for this wonderful city is an example of western thrift, ambition, and solid progress. Early the following morning, the touring party started in the two machines to spend a few days at Colorado Springs.

Without loss of time they drove to the famous Hot Springs, and then on through the picturesque estate of General Palmer, the founder of Colorado City. His place was copied after the well-known English castle Blenheim, and Julie was deeply impressed with the architecture of the building.

"Girls, to-morrow morning I want you to see the sun rise from the vantage point of Pike's Peak, so we won't climb that to-day. But we will go to Manitou, where the setting sun casts long-fingered shadows into the ravines, turning everything to fairy colors," said Mr. Gilroy.

The scouts were awed into silence at the grandeur of the scenery they beheld, and Mr. Gilroy said, "The Ute Indians used to come to the Manitou Waters for healing, you know. To-morrow, on your way down from the Peak, we will stop at the Ute Pass. But I want you to see the marvelous feat of engineering in this modern day that has made an auto drive to the top of Pike's Peak a possibility."

So very early the next morning the scouts were called, and after a hurried breakfast started out in the cars for the Peak. Having driven over the fine auto road, recently completed, to the top of the Peak, they got out to watch the sunrise. This was truly a sight worth working for. From the Peak they could see over an expanse of sixty thousand square miles of country, and when the rays of the sun began to touch up with silver places here and there on this vast stretch, the scene was most impressive.

After leaving Pike's Peak, Mr. Gilroy told the chauffeur to drive to the Ute Pass. That same day the girls visited the scenic marvels of the Garden of the Gods, the Cave of the Winds, Crystal Park, and other places.

They dined at the "Hidden Inn," which was a copy of one of the Pueblo cliff-dwellings of the Mesa Verde. This Inn is built against a cliff, and is most picturesque with its Indian collection of trophies and decorations after the Pueblo people's ideals.

They visited William's Canyon and the Narrows, with its marvelous, painted cliffs of red, purple, and green; and went to Cheyenne Mountain and the canyon with its beautiful "Seven Falls." Other places that Mr. Gilroy knew of but that were seldom listed in the guidebooks because they were out of the way, were visited and admired.

The last day of their visit to Colorado City, they all took the railroad train and went to Cripple Creek. The train wound over awesome heights, through rifts in cliffs, and past marvelously colored walls of rock, and so on to the place where more gold is mined than at any other spot in the world.

That night the scouts returned to the hotel at Colorado City well tired out, but satisfied with the touring they had accomplished in the time they had been in Colorado. In the morning they said good-bye to the gorgeous places in Pike's Peak Park and headed again for Denver.

A splendid road led through Pike View, where the best views of Pike's Peak can be had. Then they passed the queer formation of rock called "Monument Park," and on still further they came to a palisade of white chalk, more than a thousand feet wide and one-fifth that in height, that was known as Casa Blanca.

Castle Rock was the next place of interest passed. It is said to be a thousand feet higher than Denver. Then several picturesque little towns were passed by, and at last Fort Logan was reached. As an army post this spot interested the scouts, but Mr. Gilroy gave them no time to watch the good-looking young officers, but sped them on past Loretto, Overland, and Denver Mile, finally into Denver again.

As they drove into the city, Mr. Gilroy explained why he had to hurry them. "You see, this is almost the middle of June, and I am supposed to return from the mountains in September with reports and specimens for the Government.

"Few people tarry in the Rockies after September, as the weather is unbearable for 'Tenderfeet.' So I have to get through my work before that time. Besides, Uncle Vernon is probably now awaiting us at the hotel, and he must not be left to wander about alone, or we may lose him."

"When can we start for the Rockies, Gilly?" eagerly asked Julie, voicing the cry of all the other scouts.

"As soon as the Indian guide gives us the 'high sign,'" replied Mr. Gilroy.

"About when will that be?" insisted Julie.

"Where is he now, Gilly?" added Ruth.

"I suppose he is in Denver waiting for us, but we can tell better after we see Uncle. I wired him to meet Tally there and complete any arrangements necessary to our immediate departure from Denver the day after we get back there."

"I hope the guide's name is easier to say than Yhon's was last summer," laughed Mrs. Vernon.

"The only name I have ever given him is 'Tally'; but his correct name has about ninety-nine letters in it and when pronounced it sounds something like Talitheachee-choolee. Now can you blame me for quickly abbreviating it to Tally?" laughed Mr. Gilroy.

"I should say not!" laughed the girls, and Julie added, "Ho, Tally is great! It will constantly remind the scouts to keep their records up to date."

Mr. Vernon was found at the hotel, comfortably ensconced in a huge leather chair. He pretended to be fast asleep, but was soon roused when the lively scouts fell upon him in their endeavor to tell him how glad they were to see him again.

"Spare me, I beg, and I will lead you to the nicest meal you ever tasted!" cried he, gasping.

Mr. Gilroy laughed and added, "You'd better, for it's Tally, and wild Indian cooking hereafter, for three months!"

"That threat holds no fears for us brave scouts," retorted the Corporal.

The girls followed quickly after Mr. Vernon, just the same, when he led the way to the dining-room. Here he had his party seated in a quiet corner, and then he reported to Mr. Gilroy all he had done since he landed in Denver in the morning.

"I have the surprise of the season for the scouts, I'm thinking," began Mr. Vernon, smiling at the eager faces of the girls. "Have you formed *any* idea of how we are going to travel to the Divide?"

Even Mr. Gilroy wondered what his friend meant, for he had asked Tally to secure the best horses possible in Denver. And the scouts shook their heads to denote that they were at sea.

Mrs. Vernon laughed, "Not on foot, I trust!"

"No, indeed, my dear! Not with shoe leather costing what it does since the war," retorted Mr. Vernon.

"We all give up,—tell us!" demanded his wife.

"First I have to tell you a tale,—for thereby hangs the rest of it.

"You see, Tally came here first thing this morning, and when I came in from my train, which was an hour late from Chicago, he greeted me. I hadn't the faintest idea who he was until after the clerk gave me the wire from Gilly, then I saluted as reverently as he had done. Finally his story was told.

"It seems 'Mee'sr Gil'loy' told Tally to get outfit and all the horses, including two mules for pack-animals (although I never knew until Tally told me, that mules were horses). And poor Tally was in an awful way because he couldn't find a horse worth shucks in the city of Denver. I fancy Tally knows horseflesh and would not be taken in by the dealers, eh, Gilly?" laughed Mr. Vernon.

Mr. Gilroy nodded his head approvingly, and muttered, "He is *some* guide, I tell you!" Then Mr. Vernon proceeded with his tale.

"Well, Tally got word the other day from his only brother, who runs a ranch up past Boulder somewhere, that a large ranch-wagon, ordered and paid for several months before, was not yet delivered. Would Tally go to the wagon-factory, and urge them to ship the vehicle, as the owner was in sore need of it this summer.

"Tally had gone to the factory all right, but the boss said it was impossible to make any deliveries to such out-of-the-way ranches, and the railroad refused freight for the present. Poor Tally wired his brother immediately, and got a disconcerting reply.

"He was authorized to take the wagon away from the manufacturer and send it on by *any route* possible. But the brother did not offer any suggestions for that route, nor did he provide means by which Tally could hitch the wagon up and send it on *via* its own transportation-power or expenses.

"Fortunately for Tally, and all of us, a horse-dealer had overheard the story and now joined us. ''Scuse me fer buttin' in,' he said, 'but I got some hosses I want to ship to Boulder, and no decent driver fer 'em. Why cain't we-all hitch up our troubles an' drive 'em away. Let your Injun use my hosses as fur as Boulder, and no charge to him. He drives the animals to a stable I'll mention and c'lect fer feed and expenses along the road, but no pay fer himself,—that's squared on the use my beasts give you-all.'

"I ruminated. Here we were with Tally who had a wagon on his hands and no horses, and here was a dealer with four horses and no wagon. It sure seemed a fine hitch to make, so we all hitched together. So now we are all starting early in the morning *via* a prairie schooner to Boulder. How do you like it?"

A cry of mingled excitement and delight soon told him what the scouts thought of the plan, but Mr. Gilroy remarked, "But what am I to do about horses for the rest of the jaunt?"

"Oh, Tally says he can drive much better bargains with ranchers than in the city here, and the horses trained for mountain climbing by the ranchers are far superior to the hacks that have been used for years to trot about Denver City. So I decided to put it right up to Tally, and he agreed to supply splendid mounts for each one of us, or guide you free of charge all summer," said Mr. Vernon.

CHAPTER TWO
VIA A "PRAIRIE SCHOONER"

Imagination had painted for the scouts a most thrilling ride in a prairie schooner, but they learned to their sorrow that the great ranch wagon built for travel over the heavy western roads and rough trails, was not quite as luxurious as a good automobile, going on splendid eastern state roads.

Ranch wagons are manufactured to withstand all sorts of ditches and obstructions in western roadways. They are constructed with great stiff springs, and the wheels have massive steel bands on still more massive rims. Into such a vehicle were packed the baggage and camping outfits that were meant to provide lodging and cooking for the party for the summer.

The four strong horses, which were to be delivered to a dealer in Boulder, pulled the wagon. Tally understood well how to drive a four-in-hand, but the going was not speedy, accustomed as the passengers were to traveling in fast automobiles.

Tally took the direct road to Boulder because it was the best route to the Rocky Mountain National Park, where Mr. Gilroy wished to examine certain moraines to find specimens he needed for his further work.

The wagon had rumbled along for several hours, and the tourists were now in the wonderful open country with the Rockies frowning down upon them from distant great heights, while the foothills into which they were heading were rising before them.

The road they were on ran along a bald crest of one of these foothills. Turning a bend in the trail, the scouts got their first glimpse of a genuine cattle-ranch. It was spread out in the valley between two mountains, like a table set for a picnic. The moving herd of cattle and the cowboys looked like dots on the tablecloth.

"Oh, look, every one! What are those tiny cowboys doing to the cattle?" called Julie, eagerly pointing to a mass of steers which were being gathered together at one corner of the range.

"I verily believe they are working the herd, Vernon! What say you,—shall we detour to give the scouts an idea of how they do it?" asked Mr. Gilroy.

Mr. Vernon took the field glasses and studied the mass for a few moments, then said, "To be sure, Gilroy! I'd like to watch the boys do it, too."

"I have never witnessed the sight, although we all have heard about it," added Mrs. Vernon. "It will be splendid to view such a scene as we travel along."

Mr. Gilroy then turned to the driver. "Tally, when we reach the foot of this descent, take a trail that will lead us past that ranch where the cowboys are working cattle out of the herd."

Tally nodded, and at the first turn he headed the horses towards the ranch a few miles away. When the tourists passed the rough ranch-house of logs, a number of young children ran out to watch the party of strangers, for visitors in that isolated spot were a curiosity.

The guide reined in his horses upon a knoll a short distance from the scene where the cattle were being rounded up. Spellbound, the scouts watched the great mass of the broad brown backs of the restless cattle, with their up-thrusting, shining horns constantly tossing, or impatient heads swaying from side to side. All around the vast herd were cowboys, picturesque in sombreros, and chaps with swinging ropes coiled ready to "cut out" a certain steer. Meanwhile, threading in and out of the concentrated mass, other horsemen were driving the cattle to the edge of the round-up.

"What do they intend doing with those they lasso, Gilly?" asked Joan.

"They will brand them with the ranch trade-mark, and then ship them to the large packing-houses."

Mrs. Vernon managed to get several fine photographs of the interesting work, and then the Indian guide was told to drive on. Seeking for a way out to the main trail again, Tally ascended a very steep grade. Upon reaching the top, the scouts were given another fine view of the valley on the other side of the ridge. The scene looked like a Titanic checkerboard, with its squares accurately marked off by the various farms that dotted the land. But these "dots" really were extensive ranches, as the girls learned when they drove nearer and past them.

The day had been unusually hot for the month of June in that altitude, and towards late afternoon the sky became suddenly overcast.

"Going to get wet, Tally?" asked Mr. Gilroy, leaning out to glance up at the scudding clouds.

"Much wet," came from the guide, but he kept his horses going at the same pace as before.

Thunderstorms in the Rockies do not creep up gradually. They just whoop up, and then empty the contents of their black clouds upon any place they select,—although the clouds are impartial, as a rule, in the selection of the spot.

Had the storm known that a crowd of tenderfeet were in the ranch wagon it could scarcely have produced a greater spectacle. It seemed as if all the elements combined to make impressive for the girls this, their first experience of a thunderstorm in the Rockies.

Before the sun had quite hidden behind an inky curtain, a blinding flash cleft the cloud and almost instantaneously a deafening crash followed. Even though every one expected the thunder, it startled them. In another minute's time the downpour began. Wherever water could find entrance, there the howling wind drove in the slanting rain.

"Every one huddle in the middle of the wagon—keep away from the canvas sides!" Mr. Gilroy tried to shriek to those behind him.

Flashes with the accompanying cracks of thunder followed closely one upon the other, so that no one could be heard to speak, even though he yelled at the top of his lungs. The wind rose to a regular gale and the wagon rocked like a cockleshell on a choppy sea. The Indian sat unconcerned and kept driving as if in the most heavenly day, but the four horses reared their heads, snorting with fear and lunging at the bits in nervousness.

The storm passed away just as unexpectedly as it came, but it left the road, which was at best rough and full of holes, filled with water. The wagon wheels splashed through these wells, soaking everything within a radius of ten feet, and constantly shaking the scouts up thoroughly.

"I feel like a pillow, beaten up by a good housekeeper so that the feathers will fluff up," said Julie.

"I'd rather feel like a pillow than to have my tongue chopped to bits," cried Ruth, complainingly. "If I have any tongue left after this ride, I shall pickle it for safekeeping."

"Can't Featherweight sit still?" laughed Joan.

Mrs. Vernon placed an arm about Ruth's shoulder to hold her steadier, just as an unusually deep hole shook up everybody and all the baggage in the wagon.

"There now! That's the last bite left in my tongue! Three times I thought it was bitten through, but this last jolt twisted the roots so that I will have to have an artificial one hinged on at the first hospital we find," wailed Ruth, showing the damaged organ that all might pity her.

Instead of giving sympathy, every one laughed, and Julie added, "At least your tongue is still in use, but my spine caved in at that last ravine we passed through, and now I have no backbone."

Just as the scouts began laughing merrily at the two girls the front wagon wheel on the right side dropped into a hole, while the horses strained at the traces. The awful shock and jar given the passengers threw them against the canvas sides, and then together again in a heap.

The babel of shouting, screaming, laughing voices that instantly sounded from the helpless pile of humanity frightened the nervous horses. The leaders plunged madly, but the wheel stuck fast in the hole. Tally held a stiff rein, but the leaders contaminated the two rear horses, and all four plunged, reared, snorted, and pulled different ways at once. The inevitable was sure to happen!

"Jump, Tally, and grab the leaders! I'll hold them in!" cried Mr. Gilroy, catching hold of the reins.

"Here, Gill, let me hold the reins while you help Tally!" shouted Mr. Vernon, instantly crawling over the front seat and taking the reins in hand.

So Mr. Gilroy sprang out after Tally, and made for one of the leaders while the guide caught hold of the other. But just as the Indian reached up to take the leather, the horse managed to work the bit between his teeth. At the same time, the lunging beasts yanked the wagon wheel up out of the hole, and feeling the release of what had balked their load, the horses began tearing along the road.

Tally dangled from the head of the first horse whose bit he had tried to work back into place. Mr. Vernon held firmly to the reins as he sat on the driver's seat of the wagon. But Mr. Gilroy was left clear out of sight, standing in the middle of the muddy road, staring speechlessly after the disappearing vehicle. The scouts were tossed back and forth like tennis balls, but the tossing was not done as gracefully as in a game of tennis.

Fortunately for all concerned, the road soon ascended a steep grade, and a long one. The cumbersome wagon was too heavy to be flipped up that hill without the four horses becoming breathless. The leaders were the first to heave and slow down in their pace; then the two rear beasts panted and slowed, and finally all came to a dead stop. This gave Tally his opportunity to drop from his perilous clutch and glare at the horses.

"*Outlaws!*" hissed he at the animals, as if this ignominious western term was sufficient punishment to shame the horses.

"Poor Gilly! Have we lost him?" cried Betty, who had been shaken into speechlessness during the wild ride.

Mr. Vernon took the field glasses from his pocket and focussed them along the road he had so recently flown over in the bouncing wagon. Suddenly a wild laugh shook him, and he passed the glasses to his wife.

The Captain leveled them and took a good look, then laughing as heartily as her husband, she gave them to Julie and hurriedly adjusted the camera.

The Scout Leader took them and looked. "Oh, girls! You ought to see Gilly. He is trying to hurry up the long road, but he is constantly jumping the water holes and slipping in the mud. Here—every one take a squint at him."

By the time Mr. Gilroy came up the long steep hill, every scout had had a good laugh at the appearance he made while climbing, and the Captain had taken several funny snapshots of him.

Upon reaching the wagon, Mr. Gilroy sighed, "Well, I am not sure which was worse—Tally's ride or that walk!"

"Um—him walk, badder of all!" grinned the Indian.

The scouts rolled up the side curtains of the wagon that they could admire the view as they passed. And with every one feeling resigned to a mild shaking as compared to the last capers of the four horses, the journey was resumed.

Great overhanging boulders looked ready to roll down upon and crush such pigmies as these that crawled along the road under them. Then, here and there, swift, laughing streams leaped over the rocks to fall down many, many hundreds of feet into the gorges riven between the cliffs. The falling waters sprayed everything and made of the mist a veritable bridal-veil of shimmering, shining white.

"Tally, shall we reach Boulder to-night?" asked Mr. Gilroy, gazing at the fast-falling twilight.

"Late bimeby," Tally said, shrugging his shoulders to express his uncertainty.

"Well, then, if we are going to be late, and as the way is not too smooth, I propose we pitch camp for the night. What say you?" suggested Mr. Gilroy, turning to hear the verdict of the scouts.

"Oh, that will be more fun than stopping at a hotel in Boulder!" exclaimed the Leader, the other girls agreeing with her.

"Very well, Gilly; let us find a suitable place for camp," added the Captain.

"We need not pitch the tents, as you scouts can sleep in the wagon, and we three men will stretch out beside the campfire. Tally can pull in at the first good clearing we find along the way," explained Mr. Gilroy.

"If we bunk in the wagon, we'll have to stretch out in a row," remarked Joan.

"We'll look like a lot of dolls on the shelf of a toy-shop," giggled Julie.

"I don't want to sleep next to you, Julie—you're such a kicker in your sleep," complained Betty. Everybody laughed at the sisters, and Anne said:

"I don't mind kicks, as I never feel them when I'm asleep."

Tally had brought canned and prepared food for just such an emergency as an unexpected camp; so now the supper was quickly cooked and the travelers called to enjoy it.

Night falls swiftly in the mountains, and even though the day may have been warm, the nights in the Rockies are cold. A fire is always a comfort, so when supper was over the scouts sat around the fire, thoroughly enjoying its blaze.

The late afterglow in the sky seemed to hover over the camp as if reluctant to fade away and leave the scouts in the dark. The atmosphere seemed tinged with orchid tints, and a faint, almost imperceptible white chill pervaded the woods.

"Girls," said Mr. Gilroy, "we have shelter, food and clothing enough, in this wonderful isolation of Nature—is there anything more that humans can really secure with all their struggling for supremacy? Is not this life in grand communion with Mother Nature better than the cliff-dwellers in great cities ever have?"

Mrs. Vernon agreed thoroughly with him and added, "Yes, and man can have, if he desires it, this sublime and satisfying life in the mountains, where every individual is supreme over all he surveys—as the Creator willed it to be."

Tally finished clearing away the supper, and sat down to have a smoke. But Mr. Gilroy turned to him, and said, "Tally, we would like to hear one of your tribe's legends, like those you used to tell me."

"Oh, yes, Tally! please, please!" immediately came from the group of girls.

Tally offered no protest, but removed the pipe from his lips and asked, "You like Blackfeet tale?"

"Yes, indeed!" chorused those about the fire.

"My people, Blackfeet Tribe. Him hunt buffalo, elk, and moose. Him travel far, and fight big. Tally know tribe history, an' Tally tell him."

Then he began to relate, in his fascinating English, a tale that belonged to his people. The Dandelion Scouts would have liked to write the story down in their records as Tally gave it, but they had to be satisfied with such English as they knew.

"Long ago, when the First People lived on earth, there were no horses. The Blackfeet bred great dogs for hauling and packing. Some Indians used elk for that purpose, but the wild animals were not reliable, and generally broke away when they reached maturity.

"In one of the camps of a Blackfeet Tribe lived two children, orphaned in youth. The brother was stone deaf, but the sister was very beautiful, so the girl was made much of, but the boy was ignored by every one.

"Finally the girl was adopted by a Chief who had no children, but the squaw would not have the deaf boy about her lodge. The sister begged that her brother be allowed to live with her, but the squaw was obdurate and prevailed. So the poor lad was kicked about and thrust away from every tent where he stopped to ask for bread.

"Good Arrow, which was the boy's name, kept up his courage and faith that all would still be righted for him. The sister cried for her brother's companionship until a day when the tribe moved to a new camp. Then the lad was left behind.

"Good Arrow lived on the scraps that he found in the abandoned camp until, at last, he had consumed every morsel of food. He then started along the trail worn by the moving tribe. It was not a long journey, but he had had no food for several days now, and he knew not where to find any until he reached his sister.

"He was traveling as fast as he could run, and his breath came pumping forth like gusts from an engine. The perspiration streamed from every pore, and he felt dizzy. Suddenly something sounded like a thunderclap inside his head, and he felt something snap. He placed both hands over his ears for a moment, and felt something soft and warm come out upon the palms. He looked, and to his consternation saw that a slender waxen worm had been forced from each ear.

"Then he heard a slight sound in the woods. And he realized, with joy, that he could hear at last! So distinctly could he hear, that he heard a woodmouse as it crept carefully through the grass a distance from the trail.

"Almost bursting with joy and happiness over his good news, he ran on regardless of all else. He wanted only to reach his sister and tell her.

"But that same morning the Chief, who had adopted the girl, announced to his squaw that he could not stand the memory of the lad's sad face when the tribe abandoned him. The Chief declared that he was going back and adopt the poor child, so he could be with his sister.

"In spite of his wife's anger the Chief started back, but met the boy not far down the trail. The lad cried excitedly and showed the waxen worms upon his palms in evidence of his story. The Chief embraced him and told him what he had planned to do that very day. Good Arrow was rejoiced at so much good fortune, and determined to be great, and do something courageous and brave for his Chief.

"He grew to be a fine young brave, more courageous and far more learned in all ways than any other youth in the tribe. Then one day he spoke to his Chief:

"'I want to find Medicine, but know not where to get it.'

"'Be very brave, fearless with the enemy, exceedingly charitable to all, of kind heart to rich and poor alike, and always think of others first,—then will the Great Spirit show you how to find Medicine,' replied the Chief.

"'Must I be kind to Spotted Bear? He hates me and makes all the trouble he can, in camp, for me,' returned Good Arrow.

"'Then must you love Spotted Bear, not treat him as an enemy, but turn him into a friend to you. Let me tell you his story,' said the Chief.

"'One day Spotted Bear took a long journey to a lake where he had heard of wonderful Medicine that could be had for the asking. He says he met a stranger who told him how to secure the Medicine he sought. And to prove that he had found it he wears that wonderful robe, which he claims the Great Medicine Man presented to him. He also told us, upon his return, of great dogs that carried men as easily as baggage.

"'We asked him why he had not brought back the dogs for us, and he said that they were not for us, but were used only by the gods that lived near the lake where he met the Medicine Man.'

"Good Arrow listened to this story and then exclaimed, 'I shall go to this lake and ask the Medicine Man to give me the dogs.'

"All the persuasions of his sister failed to change his determination, so he started one day, equipped for a long journey. When Spotted Bear heard that Good Arrow had gone for the dogs he had failed to bring to camp, he was furious and wanted to follow and kill the youth. The other braves restrained him, however.

"Good Arrow traveled many days and finally arrived at a lake such as had been described to him by the Chief. Here he saw an old man who asked him what he sought.

"'Knowledge and wisdom to rule my people justly.'

"'Do you wish to win fame and wealth thereby?' asked the bent-over old man.

"'I would use the gifts for the good of the tribe, to help and enlighten every one,' returned Good Arrow.

"'Ah! Then travel south for seven days and you will come to a great lake. There you will meet one who can give you the Medicine you crave. I cannot do more.'

"Then the young brave journeyed for seven days and seven nights, until, utterly exhausted, he fell upon the grass by the side of the trail. How long he slept there, he knew not; but upon awakening, he saw the great lake spread out before his eyes, and standing beside him was a lovely child of perfect form and features.

"Good Arrow smiled on the child; then the little one said, 'Come, my father said to bring you. He is waiting to welcome you.'

"With these words spoken, the child ran straight into the lake and disappeared under the water.

"Fearfully the youth ran after, to save the little one. He plunged into the deep water, thinking not of himself, but of how to rescue the babe.

"As he touched the water, it suddenly parted and left a dry trail that ran over to a wonderful lodge on the other side. He now saw the child running ahead and calling to a Chief who stood before the lodge.

"Good Arrow followed and soon met the Chief whom he found to be the Great Medicine Man he had sought. The purpose of his journey was soon explained, then the Chief beckoned Good Arrow to follow him.

"'I will show you the elk-dogs that were sent from the Great Spirit for the use of mortals. But no man has been found good enough or kind enough to take charge of them.'

"Then Good Arrow was taken to the wide prairie, where he saw the most wonderful animals feeding. They were larger than elk and had shining coats of hair. They had beautiful glossy manes and long sweeping tails. Their sensitive ears and noses were quivering in wonderment as they watched a stranger going about their domain.

"'Young man of the earth,' said the Chief, patting one of the animals that nuzzled his hand, 'these are the horses that were meant for mankind. If you wish to take them back with you it is necessary that you learn the Medicine I have prepared for you.'

"Good Arrow was thrilled at the thought that perhaps he might be the one to bring this blessing on man. He thought not of the wealth and fame such a gift would bring to him. The Chief smiled with pleasure.

"'Ah, you have passed the first test well. This offer to you, that might well turn a great Chief's head, only made you think of the good it would bring to the children of earth. It is well.'

"So every lesson given Good Arrow was not so much for muscular power or physical endurance, but tests of character and moral worth. The youth passed these tests so creditably that the Chief finally said, 'My son, you shall return to your people with this great gift from the Spirit, if you pass the last test well.'

"'Journey three days and three nights without stopping, and *do not once turn to look back*! If you turn, you shall instantly be transformed into a dead tree beside the trail. Obey my commands, and on the third night you shall hear the hoofs of the horses who will follow you.

"'Leap upon the back of the first one that comes to you, and all the others will follow like lambs to to the camp you seek.

"'Now let me present you with a token from myself. This robe is made for Great Medicine Chiefs,' and as he spoke the Chief placed a mantle like his own over Good Arrow's shoulders. And in his hand he placed a marvelous spear.

"Good Arrow saw that the robe was exactly like the one worn by Spotted Bear, but he asked no questions about it. When the Chief found the young brave was not curious, he smiled, and said, 'Because you did not question me about Spotted Bear, I will tell you his story, that you may relate it again to the tribe and punish him justly for his cowardice.

"'Spotted Bear reached the lake where the child stood, but he would not follow her into the water,—not even to rescue her, when she cried for help. He was driven back by evil spirits, and when he found the old man who had sent him onward to find the elk-dogs, he beat him and took away his robe. That is the robe he now wears, but I permitted him to wear it until a brave youth should ask questions regarding its beauty,—then will it have accomplished its work. You are the youth, and now you hear the truth about Spotted Bear. Judge righteous judgment upon him, and do not fear to punish the crime.

"'Now, farewell, Good Arrow. You are worthy to guide my horses back to mortals. The robe will never wear out, and the spear will keep away all evil spirits and subdue your enemies.'

"When Good Arrow would have thanked the Chief, he found he was alone upon the shore where he first saw the child. Had it not been for the gorgeous robe upon his back and the spear in his hand, he would have said it was all a dream from which he had but just awakened.

"He turned, as he had been commanded, and straightway journeyed along the trail. He went three days and three nights before he heard a living thing. Then the echoes of hoofbeats thudded on the trail after him. But he turned not.

"Soon afterward, a horse galloped up beside him, and as he leaped upon its back, it neighed. The others followed after the leader, and all rode into camp, as the great Chief had said it would be.

"Great was the wonderment and rejoicing when Good Arrow showed his people the marvelous steeds and told his story. The robe and spear bore him out in his words. But Spotted Bear turned to crawl away from the campfire. Then Good Arrow stood forth, and said in a loud voice of judgment, 'Bring Spotted Bear here for trial.'

"The story of his cowardice and theft was then related to the tribe, and the judgment pronounced was for the outcast to become a nameless wanderer on the earth. Even as the Chief spoke these words of punishment, the robe he had always bragged about, fell from his back and turned into dust at his feet.

"Thus came the Spirit's gift of horses to mankind, and Good Arrow became a wise Medicine Man of the Blackfeet."

Tally concluded his story, and resumed his pipe as if there had been no prolonged lapse between his smokes.

CHAPTER THREE
JULIE'S STRANGE EXPERIENCE

"That was a splendid story, Tally," said the Captain, as Tally concluded his legend.

"Yes, I like it better than those I have read of the First Horses in books from the Smithsonian Institution," added Mrs. Vernon.

"Him true story! My Chief tell so," declared Tally, positively, and not one of the scouts refuted his statement.

"Well, I don't know how you girls feel, but I will confess that I'm ready for a nap," remarked Mr. Gilroy, trying to hide a yawn.

"No objections heard to that motion," declared Mr. Vernon.

"Not after such a day's voyage in this schooner," laughed Julie. "I'll be fast asleep in a jiffy."

So the blankets were spread out over the floor of the wagon, and the girls rolled themselves into them, and stretched out as planned. The planks of the floor were awfully hard and there seemed to be ridges just where they were not wanted. Directly under Julie's back was a great iron bolt but she could not move far enough to either one side or the other to avoid it. So she doubled her blanket over it, and left her feet upon the bare wooden planks.

"I'm thankful there are no tall members in this Troop," remarked the Captain, after they were all settled in a row. "If there were, her feet would have to hang over the side of the wagon."

Tally and the two men spread out their rubber covers in front of the fire, and all were soon asleep.

Julie's brag about falling fast asleep in a jiffy proved false, for she could not rest comfortably because of the bolt. So her sleep was troubled and she half-roused several times, although she did not fully awaken. Then, during one of these drowsy experiences when she tried to get on one side of the bolt, she heard a strange sound.

She sat up and looked around. It was still dark, although the first streaks of dawn were showing in the sky. Her companions were stretched out under their covers, and Mrs. Vernon was softly snoring. Julie lifted a corner of the canvas curtain to ascertain what it was that awakened her, and she saw a suspicious sight.

The guide was in the act of getting upon his feet without disturbing the two men who slept soundly by the fireside. He waved a hand, as a signal, towards the brush some ten feet away. And there Julie saw a hand and arm motioning him, but no other part of its owner could be seen.

"Well I never!" thought Julie to herself, as she watched Tally creep away from the fire and make for the bushes.

He was soon hidden behind the foliage, and then Julie heard sounds as of feet moving along the forest trail.

"I'm not going to let him put anything over on us, if I know it!" thought she. And she quickly stepped over the quiet forms in the wagon, and slid down from the back of the schooner. That night the scouts had on moccasins, fortunately, and her feet made no sound as she swiftly followed the Indian through the screen of leaves. Then she saw, some dozen yards ahead of her, two forms hurrying up a steep trail that ran through the forest. One was Tally, and his companion was an Indian maiden.

Unseen, Julie softly followed after them, and finally they came to a roaring mountain torrent that was bridged by a great fallen pine. On the other side of this stream were two shining black horses, with manes and tails so long and thick that the scout marveled. They were caparisoned in Indian fashion with gay colors and fancy trappings.

The maiden quickly loosed the steeds and Tally sprang up into one saddle, while the squaw got up into the other. Then they continued up along the trail without as much as a glance behind.

Julie managed to creep over the treetrunk and gained the other side of the torrent, then ran after them as fast as she could go. But they had disappeared over the crest and the scout had to slow up, as her breath came in panting gasps.

Finally she, too, reached the summit, but there was no sign of horses or riders. A wide cleared area covered the top of the mountain, from which a marvelous view of Denver and its environs could be had. Distant peaks now glimmered in the rising sun, and Julie sighed in ecstasy at such a wonderful sight.

Then she remembered what brought her there, and she ran across the clearing to look for a trail down the other side and, perchance, a glimpse of the Indians.

Passing a screen of thick pines, she suddenly came to an old flower garden, and on the other side of it stood a rambling old stone castle, similar to Glen Eyrie at Colorado Springs.

"Humph! This looks as if some one tried to imitate General Palmer's gorgeous castle, but gave it up in despair," thought she.

Julie walked across the intervening space and reached the moss-grown stone steps that led to a great arched doorway. She had a glance, through wide-opened doors, of gloomy hallway and a great staircase, then she skirted the wing of the building, and came out to a wide terrace that ran along the entire front of the pile. The view from this high terrace caused her to stand perfectly still and gaze in awe.

She could see for miles and miles over the entire country from the height she stood upon. It was almost as wonderful a view as that from Pike's Peak. Sheer down from the stone terrace dropped a precipice of more than five thousand feet. Far down at its base she could see a stream winding a way between dots of ranches and narrow ribbons of roadways.

"This is the most marvelous scene yet!" murmured Julie. Then she frowned as a thought came to her. "If Tally knew of this place,—and it is evident that he did,—why did he not tell us of it, so that we could climb up and see it in the morning? And why isn't this old castle on the road-map, with a note telling tourists of the magnificent view from this height?"

After a long time given to silent admiration of the country as seen from the terrace, Julie turned and slowly walked up the stone steps that led into the hall. "Wonder if the place is abandoned," thought she, peeping inside the doorway.

As no sound or sign of life was evident, she tiptoed in and gazed about. The tiles on the floor were of beautiful design and coloring, and the woodwork was tinted to correspond. The walls were covered with rare old tapestries, while here and there adown the length of the hall stood suits of armor and mailed figures.

Bronze chandeliers hung from the high ceilings, and on each side of the hall stood bronze *torchères* holding gigantic wax candles.

"Well, in all my life I never dreamed of visiting such a museum of old relics!" sighed Julie, who dearly loved antiques.

Suddenly, as silently as everything else about the place, there appeared a white-haired servitor in baronial uniform. He came forward and deferentially bowed, then he spoke to Julie.

"Are you the Indian maiden the guide was to meet to-day?"

Julie was so amazed at the question that she could not reply, so she barely nodded her head.

"Then follow me, as the master waits. The guide sits below, eating breakfast," added the old servant.

At the mention of breakfast, Julie felt her empty stomach yearn for a bite of it, but she silently turned and followed the major-domo, as she knew him to be, along the hall and up the stairs. As they reached the first landing the old man said, "The master is in his laboratory in the tower. Breakfast will be served there."

Julie accepted this as cheerful news, so she fearlessly followed after the guide. She had seen no tower from the outside of the rambling building, but, she thought, there might have been one at the wing opposite the one around which she came when she walked to the front of the place.

Having reached the top of the stairs, Julie saw that the entire second-floor walls were covered with ancient portraits. She would have loved to stop and study the ancient costumes of the women, but the man ascended the second flight of stairs, and she must follow.

They went along the hall on the third floor, and at the end the servitor entered a small room that was heavily hung with velour *portières*. He pushed them aside and turned a knob that seemed to be set in the carved panel. Instantly this panel swung open and disclosed a narrow spiral stairway leading to an iron platform overhead.

Julie began to question the wisdom of this reckless act of hers; but having come so far, how could she back out gracefully? Why should this master want to breakfast with an Indian squaw—for such he was expecting?

"This way," politely reminded the old man, and Julie had to see the thing through to the end—whatever that might be.

At the head of these spiral stairs the man pulled on a heavy cord, and another hidden door set in carved panelling opened. Through this they went, and then the man said:

"Be seated, and I will call the master."

Julie gazed about her in profound curiosity. The room was an octagon-shaped laboratory, so dark that its corners were in shadow. The only light came from a huge glass dome ceiling. One side of the room was taken up by a great fireplace; opposite this stood a high cabinet filled with the vials and other equipment of a chemist. The paneled door through which she came took up the third side, and the five other sides were filled with tiers of shelves, where stood rows of morocco-bound books.

Great leather chairs stood about the room, and in the center, upon a magnificent Kirmanshaw rug, stood an onyx table with a great crystal globe upon it. At one side, near the narrow door through which the old servant had gone, stood a grand piano.

Julie had no time for further inspection of the room, as a unique figure suddenly appeared in the small doorway through which the servitor had gone. He was very tall and thin, and was clad in wonderfully embroidered East Indian robes. A fez cap covered the bald head on top, and a thin straggly white beard fringed the lower part of his face. Upon his scrawny finger a strange stone glittered and instantly attracted her gaze.

Julie wondered who this unusual person might be, but he vouchsafed no information. In fact, he stood perfectly still as if waiting for her to open the conversation. This proved to be the fact, for he gazed searchingly at the girl, and then murmured, "Well?"

Julie tried to summon a smile and act nonchalant, but the entire atmosphere of the place was too oppressive for such an air, so she stood, changing her weight from one foot to the other. This form of action—or to be more exact, inaction—continued for a few minutes, then the old man gave vent to a hollow laugh. It sounded so sepulchral that Julie shivered with apprehension.

He started to cross the room. When he came within a few feet of his guest he said, raspingly, "Maiden, I know thee. Thou'rt a descendant of Spotted Bear, the coward! And I—I am the young Medicine Man who won the robe and spear, and brought the horses to earth for mankind to use. Hast aught to say to that?"

At these words Julie was too amazed to answer. To see the hero of that wonderful Indian legend standing before her eyes—but oh, how old he must be, for that happened ages ago, and his yellow parchment-like skin attested to a great age.

As she thought over these facts, she could not keep her eyes from the old man's face, and now she actually could trace a resemblance to the young guide, Tally. Could the latter be a descendant of this Medicine Man's? As if the old fellow read her thoughts, he chuckled, "Aye! The guide is one of my tribe, and thou art a member of that of the outcast, Spotted Bear. Because I have found thee, I shall see that no descendant of that coward's goes forth again to trouble the world."

Julie began to fear that she had been very indiscreet in coming into this old ruin as she had done, especially as she would find it difficult to convince this old man that she was not the Indian maiden he thought her to be. But she paid attention to his next act, which was to pull out a great chair and drop back in it as if too weary to stand longer upon his spindling legs.

"Art hungry? Even my enemy must not complain of our bounty." So saying, the old man reached forth a long thin arm and his fingers pushed upon a button in the wall. Instantly a panel moved back and disclosed a cellaret built into the wall. Here were delicious fruits, cakes, and fragrant coffee.

"Help thyself. I will wait till thou art done," said he, waving his hand at the food.

Julie was so hungry that the sight of the fruit made her desperate. Had her future welfare depended upon it, she could not have withstood the temptation to eat some of that fruit. She went over to take an orange, but a horrible thrust in her back caused her to cry out and put both hands behind her.

To her horror she found the old man had thrown some hard knob at her and it had made such a dent in her flesh that it could be distinctly felt at the base of her spine. The insane laughter that greeted her wail of pain made her realize that she was in the presence of a madman!

"Why not eat, Maiden? I will amuse myself, meantime," said the old man, as he finished his laughter.

Julie saw him rise and hobble over to the piano, then seat himself before the keyboard and begin to play the weirdest music she had ever heard. But the pain in her back continued so that the thought of breakfast vanished. All she cared for now was to get rid of that suffering.

When she could stand the agony no longer, she gathered courage enough to limp over to the piano and beg him to release her, as she was in great pain.

"Aha! Didst ever think of how Spotted Bear caused the child to suffer when it went down in the water?" asked he, suspending his hands over the piano keys.

"But I hadn't anything to do with that! Why strike me for his crimes?" retorted Julie, gaining courage in her pain.

The old man frowned at her fiercely, and mumbled, "Art obstinate? Then we'll have to use other ways." He turned and pushed another button in the wall back of the piano, and instantly the glass dome overhead became darkened, so that Julie could not see the objects in the room very plainly.

The host got up and started slowly for Julie. His eyes seemed afire with a maniac's wildness, and the scout feared he was planning to attack her. She screamed for help, and ran for the door in the paneling through which she had entered. But the cry seemed muffled in her throat and no audible sound came forth.

The host laughed that same horrible laugh again, and Julie tried again, harder than ever, to shout for help. Still her vocal chords seemed paralyzed, and no sound was heard from them.

Just as she reached the paneling, the old man must have hurled another hard ball at her, for she felt the blow in her back and shrunk with the pain. And as she squirmed, she distinctly felt the painful object move from one side of her spine to the other, as if it were a button under the skin that was movable.

But the door in the panel could not be opened, and Julie worked her hands frantically over its surface, while the old Indian laughed and crept closer to her. When he was near enough to reach out and take her in his awful hands, the scout gathered all her courage and flung herself upon him.

She fought with hands and teeth, and kicked with her feet, hoping that his great age would render him too weak to resist her young muscular strength. She knew she must overpower him or he would kill her, mistaking her for the maiden descended from Spotted Bear.

She had thus far won the hand-to-hand fight, so that he was down upon his knees and she was over him with her hands at his throat, when suddenly he collapsed, and his eyes rolled upwards at her. In her horror she managed to yell for help, and then she heard—

"Julie! Julie! Have mercy! Stop tearing Betty to bits!"

Through a vague distance Julie recognized the voice of Joan. Oh, if they were only there to help! But she kept a grip on the old Chief's neck while she waited to answer the call.

Then she heard very plainly, "For the love of Pete, Julie, wake up, won't you!" And some one shook her madly.

Julie sat up and rubbed her eyes dazedly, while the scouts about her laughed wildly, and Betty scolded angrily.

"Oh, Julie, what an awful nightmare you must have had," laughed Mrs. Vernon.

"Is Tally back?" asked Julie.

"He's cooking breakfast,—smell it," said Anne, smacking her lips.

"I can smell coffee," mumbled Julie, still unconvinced that she had been dreaming. "It smells exactly like that old man's."

"What old man?" again asked the circle about her.

"Why, Good Arrow, to be sure! He lives up on that hill—and, girls, he's as old as Methusaleh, I'm sure!" declared Julie.

The wild laughter that greeted this serious statement of hers did more to rouse the Leader from a cloudy state of mind than anything else, and soon she was up and out of the wagon to look for a trail that might run over the crest of the hill.

But there was no trail, neither was there a mountain climb such as she remembered in her dreams. At breakfast, she told the dream, to the intense amusement of every one, Tally included. Then the Indian guide remarked, "No better sleep on iron bolt, nex' time!"

CHAPTER FOUR
GOING UP!

"I hope we can say good-by to the old wagon to-day," said the Captain, after they were seated again, ready to resume the journey.

"You seem not to like our luxurious schooner?" laughed Mr. Gilroy.

"Luxurious! Had we but known what this ride would be like I venture to say every scout would have chosen to walk from Denver," exclaimed Mrs. Vernon.

"And here I've been condemning myself as being the only ingrate in the party!" returned Mr. Gilroy. "I remember with what enthusiasm the scouts hailed the suggestion of traveling *a la* prairie schooner."

As the wagon came out from the screen of trees where they had camped for the night, the scouts saw the vapors in the valley eddy about and swiftly vanish in the penetrating gleams from the rising sun. Here and there patches of vivid green lay revealed, but in another half hour the sun would be strong enough, with the aid of a stiff breeze, to dispel all the clinging mists of night into their native nothingness.

"Just as our earthly pains and sorrows go," remarked Mrs. Vernon.

"Yes, Verny, just like Julie's dream, eh? She woke up and could hardly believe that she was here—safe and happy," added Joan.

The road was rough and the joggling was as bad as ever, but the scouts were not so resigned as they had been the day before. Every little while they asked, "*Now* how far are we from Boulder?" for there they would have surcease from such "durance vile" as this mode of travel imposed upon them.

To distract their attention from physical miseries, Mr. Vernon asked a question, knowing that Mr. Gilroy would instantly divine his intention and follow it up.

"Gilroy, how do you explain the queer fact that the higher we go on these grand heights, the more stunted we find the trees? One would expect to find beautiful timber on top."

The scouts listened with interest, and Mr. Gilroy noted this and consequently took the cue given him.

"Why, timber-line in the West, Vernon, means more than the end of the forest growth. Most trees near the top of the peaks are stunted by the cold, or are twisted by the gales, and become bent or crippled by the fierce battles they have to wage against the elements. But they are not vanquished—oh, no!

"These warriors of the forests seem to realize with a fine intelligence how great is their task. They must protect the young that grow on the sides further down the mountain; they must hold back the destroying powers of the storm, that the *grand* and *beautiful* scions of this forest family be not injured. They have learned, through many courageous engagements with Nature's fierce winters, that the post appointed them in life can never offer them soft and gentle treatment while there remains such work as theirs to do, work that needs tried strength and brave endurance.

"I have never found a coward growing in the ranks of the closely-linked, shoulder-to-shoulder front of trees that mark the timber-line. Although they may not *seem* to grow, materially, more than from eight to twelve feet high, and though many look deformed by the overwhelming conditions, so that they present strange shapes in comparison with the erect tall giants down the mountainside, yet I love to remember that in His perfect Creation, these same fighters have won greatness and eternal beauty for their service to others.

"In most cases, you will find that the higher the altitude of the peak and the wilder the winds, the closer grow the trees, as if to find increase of strength in the one united front that they present to the storms. These winter gales are so powerful that they tear at every object offering resistance to their destructive force. Thus the limbs growing on the outer side of the trees on timber-line are all torn away, or twisted back upon the parent trunk.

"But there are times when even the most valiant defenders of the forest are momentarily overpowered. There comes a blizzard; the gale howls and shrieks as it tears back and forth for days at a stretch, trying to force a passage through the defence line. And sometimes a little soldier is rooted up with malignant fury, and used by the merciless gale to batter at his companions. This generally proves futile, however.

"It is not always in the wintertime that the most terrific blizzards occur in the Rockies. In July, when all the country is pining for a breeze, these peaks produce blizzards that surpass anything heard of in winter, and these summer storms are the most destructive, as the trees are green and full of tender tips, that are ruthlessly torn off during the gale.

"Then, too, the summer months generally produce the awful snowslides you hear about, that are quite common in the Rockies."

"Oh, I wish we could see one of them!" exclaimed Julie, impulsively.

"Child, you don't know what you are saying!" said Mr. Gilroy, earnestly. "If you ever went through one, as I have, you'd never want to experience another, I assure you."

"Oh, Gilly! Do tell us about it," cried the scouts.

And Mr. Vernon added, "Yes, Gilroy, do tell us the story."

"It was many years ago, while I was on a geological trip through the Rockies. Tally and I were ready to start for a several days' outing on the peaks when the man we lodged with said, 'You are going out at a bad time. Some big slides have been reported recently.'

"I, like Julie here, said, 'I'd like the excitement of riding a slide.'

"The rancher said I was locoed, but he went about his business after that. So I took my snowshoes in case I met a slide and had to ride it.

"Tally and I were soon climbing the trail, and as we went higher and higher, I felt pleasantly excited to see several small slides start from distant peaks and ride ruthlessly over everything to gain a resting-place.

"Then we both heard a rumble and stood looking about. We now beheld a slide quite close at hand—on our own ridge but on the far side. It coasted slowly at first, but gathered momentum as it went, until it was flying downwards.

"It was about fifty feet wide and several hundred feet long, but it cut a clean channel through the forest, carrying great trees, rocks, and other objects on its crest. Before it had traveled five hundred yards, it had gathered into its capacious maw tons of débris, besides the vast blanket of snow it started out with. All this made a resistless force that swept over other forest impedimenta, dragging all along with its flood.

"It looked as if the village that snuggled at the foot of the mountain would be completely smothered and destroyed, when suddenly, the entire river of white was deflected by an erosion that had cut a wayward pathway across the mountainside. This attracted the slide down into the ravine. And as its mass went over the edge of the gulch, fine powdery particles filled the air, but nothing more than a dull, grinding sound rose to me as a tremor shook the ground, and I realized that it had found its end in the canyon.

"Upon my return to the ranch, I was told that that slide had cut down and ruined fifty thousand fine trees. Nothing could be done with them after such a battle with the slide.

"But the next day, as I still thrilled with the memory of the immense slide, I heard a rumbling sound just above where we were. Tally screamed, 'Look out. She come!'

"I saw snow sliding across a shallow depression above, and heading straight for me. Tally had managed to scramble quickly out of the way, and I worked those snowshoes faster than anything I ever did before or since—believe me!

"Before I could reach a safety zone, however, I was caught in the outer edge of the avalanche and whirled along for some distance. By dint of working those same snowshoes I managed to gain the extreme edge, where I flung myself recklessly out into space, not knowing where I might land.

"Fortunately, I was left sprawling with legs and arms about a pine, while the slide rioted on without me. I lifted my bruised head because I wished to see all I could of it, and I was able to witness the havoc it wrought in its descent. When it reached the bottom of the mountain it collided with a rocky wall on an opposite cliff. The first meeting of the snow with this powerful resistance curled it backward upon itself, while the rest of the slide piled up on top, and quickly filled the narrow valley with its débris.

"Had I not been so near the line of least suction, or had I been in the middle of that fearful slide, nothing could have saved me. I should have been buried under tons of snow even if I survived a death-dealing blow from a rock or tree during the descent.

"Now, Julie, do you still care to experience a hand-to-hand battle with a slide?"

"If it wasn't for all such thrilling adventures, Gilly, you wouldn't be so entertaining. When one is in the Rockies, one looks for experiences that go *with* the Rockies," declared the girl.

Mr. Gilroy shook his head as if to say Julie was hopeless. But Joan laughingly remarked, "A snowslide wouldn't be any wilder than Julie's visit to old man Good Arrow in his castle."

"And about as frightful as the pit he would have thrown Julie into," added Mr. Gilroy.

"Joking aside, Scouts. We expect to meet with various thrilling adventures during our sojourn in the Rockies, and I don't believe one takes such dire risks if one is careful," said Julie.

"Maybe not, but you are not careful. In fact, you take 'dire risks' every time," retorted Mr. Gilroy.

Nothing was said for a few minutes, then Tally spoke, "Mees'r Gilloy—him come to Boulder, pooty quick!"

"Ha, that's good news!" remarked Mr. Vernon.

"Yes, and our little scheme worked fine, eh, Uncle," laughed Mr. Gilroy. But all the coaxings from the scouts could not make either man say what that scheme had been.

At Boulder the party gladly left the wagon for Tally to deliver to his brother, and the horses were turned over to the man they were intended for. While Tally was waiting for his brother's arrival, Mr. Gilroy found he could conduct his party through the Boulder Canyon, known as "The Switzerland Trail."

So they got on a train and rode through a canyon which, as the name suggested, was everywhere lined with great boulders of all shapes and sizes. Here a roaring torrent would cleave a way down to the bottom of the canyon, while there an abrupt wall of rock defied the elements and all things else to maintain its stand.

At Tungsten, the end of the trail, the scouts visited the district where this metal is mined. When they were through with the visit, Mr. Gilroy told the girls that Boulder County's record of income from tungsten alone was more than five million dollars a year.

The State University at Boulder was visited upon the return of the scout tourists to that city. Here the girls learned that the campus covered over sixty acres of ground, and that the university boasted of twenty-two splendidly equipped buildings, equal to any in the world. It also had a library of its own that numbered about eighty-three thousand volumes. The value of the buildings approximated one million, seven hundred and fifty thousand dollars.

"It doesn't seem possible, when you look around at what this place is—or seems to be!" exclaimed Ruth.

"Which goes to prove that appearances are not necessarily harmonious with facts," returned Mrs. Vernon, smilingly.

When they met Tally, who was waiting at the place appointed, Julie asked, "Where do we go from here, Gilly?"

"We'll follow Tally, as he seems to have a plan back of that grin," returned Mr. Gilroy.

Every one turned to look at Tally, who in turn seemed quite taken by surprise, as he said, "Tally no plan!"

"Ah, Tally! Will you never understand my winks!" sighed Mr. Gilroy. "I wanted you to help me out while I evaded an issue with these dreadful Scouts."

"Um, Tally glad to if Mees'r Gilloy onny tell him."

The others laughed at this guileless confession, and Mr. Gilroy shook his head despairingly. Then he said, "Well, I suppose I must 'fess up.'"

"Of course, if you have any hidden schemes back in *your* brain," Julie retorted.

"This is it! Tally heard of a number of excellent horses to be had from a rancher near Loveland, so rather than wait about here for him to go and bring them back, we will go on to Loveland by train, and start from that place to ride through the Rocky Mountain National Park.

"You see, my first plan is entirely upset by a prairie schooner, an Indian, and a horse-dealer. I had expected to ride from Denver on horses secured there, and go to Ward. Then on across the Divide and so on to Hot Sulphur Springs and Steamboat Springs. But it seems the itinerary revised itself,—and it may turn out to be a good improvement on mine," said Mr. Gilroy.

"How far is the Continental Divide from Loveland?" asked Joan.

"That all depends on how far we want it to be," laughed Mr. Vernon. "One can get there in no time, or one can stop at all the attractive points along the trail and spend weeks reaching the Divide."

Then Mr. Gilroy added, "I propose leaving Loveland by an old Indian Trail Tally knows of, and thus reach Estes Park. We will take in Long's Peak on the way, and then ride on to the Divide, stopping to climb any peak we think interesting, or visit any park or moraine along the route."

So the party reached Loveland, where Tally bargained shrewdly with a rancher for the horses and two mules for the tourists. Naturally the rancher wished to sell his horses outright, but Tally convinced him how much better an arrangement it would be for all concerned to rent the animals for the season, leaving a cash security deposited with a bank to cover the loss in case any or all of the horses were lost or injured on the way. If all were returned to the rancher in good condition, Mr. Gilroy would receive his deposit back.

This entire section of Colorado was created a National Park by Congress, in January, 1915. And Estes Park is to the National Park what a beauty patch is to the face of a belle—the point of attraction that focuses the eye of the admirer.

This National Park offers plenty of room for more than a million campers, without one being so near his neighbor as to give a sense of encroachment. For those Americans who love the untrammeled life of the woods, this park provides wonderful trout streams; flora and fauna most surprising and beautiful; and not only plains, valleys, ravines, and mountain peaks as diverting places to visit, but lakes, rivers, falls, and every ideal spot of Nature that one craves to see.

In this National Park you may come unexpectedly upon a caribou grazing on the luscious grass, or in spring you may find a doting she-bear, leading her cubs to feast on the tender green shoots. But let your boots make the slightest noise, both these wild creatures will disappear so suddenly that you will rub your eyes to make sure you are awake. Other furred and feathered inhabitants of the forests will sit, screened behind the foliage and fern, laughing silently at your amateur ways of discovering them.

You may not be woodsman enough ever to spy them, but they are about, just the same. Furtive eyes will watch your every movement as you ride along the trail. The partridge that has effaced himself by merging his mottled feathers with the shaggy bark where he is hidden, saw every least thing you did. The wild hare, covered with tall grasses and fern, flicked his long ears in fun, when your awkward steps passed within an inch of his nose, and you never dreamed of his sitting there! The squirrels and woodchucks wondered at your clumsy ways in the wilderness. Did they not leap and run joyously without a sound? And you only have two feet to manage while they have four! In short, every denizen of the forest about you will know as if the message were flashed by wire, that a mere MAN is on his way through their domains.

The Park realm stretches along on the mountain top at an altitude of nine thousand feet, and more. And it embraces the most rugged section of the Continental Divide. Long's Peak rises about fourteen thousand two hundred feet high, and towers above the park plateau. It looks down upon ten or more other peaks that are only thirteen thousand feet high, and many more of twelve thousand feet altitude. Long's Peak is rocky and not easy to climb, but perfectly safe for man or beast. It is also free from the treacherous ice and snow that so often causes slides. Hence one can reach its summit, where a view of over a hundred miles of country is to be had. The Park is about twenty-five miles long and from ten to twenty miles wide.

This, then, was the wonderful place the scouts of Dandelion Troop were to visit and glory in.

CHAPTER FIVE
HITTING THE TRAIL

The horses Tally had contracted for were all the tourists could desire. They were sure-footed and experienced mountain climbers; they could go without food or water for a longer period than ordinary animals, as they had been so accustomed. They were not heavy, but wiry and muscular,—in short, the genuine ranch horse of the Rocky Mountains. The two pack mules, named Frolic and Jolt, were sleepy-looking beasts, but it was only in appearance. Once they started on the trail they proved splendid carriers, even though they took life their own way.

The little cavalcade left the hotel at Loveland the center of curious eyes, for the summer tourists stopping at the inn had heard of the well-known geologist and the Troop of Scouts. As few members of the interesting organization of Girl Scouts had ever been through the Rockies, this Troop created quite a diversion for visitors.

Tally soon turned from the beaten track that most tourists take in going to Estes Park, and led his party to the old abandoned Indian Trail. Finally they came to a cool shadowy thread of a path that could be distinguished only because the trees were not closely interlocked each with the others.

At this hour the forest was like the translucence of the sea, bathing everything in the cool green light of its depths; and the exhilarating effect was the same as the salt tang of an ocean bath.

"Makes one feel as if one were in church at Vesper time," softly declared Julie, glancing at the arched aisles they were riding through.

"Was ever cathedral so solemn, so beautiful, as this of Nature?" replied Mrs. Vernon, in a reverent tone.

Then for another long period all was silence again, as the scouts rode along, breathing in the beauty of the "silent places." When they had traveled about ten miles along this secret trail, with its ever-changing panorama of scenes, the swishing of a stream was heard. Soon after, the riders came to tumbling waters, that seemed in haste to go over the cliff that caused them to fall into a shadowy pool far below. Great rocks, overhanging pines, and gorgeous flora edged both sides of the waterfall, making a picture impossible to describe.

They descended the steep declivity that skirted the falls and picked up the trail again at the bottom. Here the scouts found several brooks that ran from the pool, but that were entirely separated from the main stream. Tally examined these canals carefully, and then held up a hand for attention.

"Scout hear beaver work? Dis beaver-canal."

"Oh, really!" whispered the girls, excitedly. "If we could only watch them at work!"

They distinctly heard the "tap, tap, tap" of something softly thudding against wood, while Tally leaned over to speak.

"Mebbe kin see beaver. Leave horse tie here, an' follow Tally sof'ly to colony. But make some noise an' beaver dive home."

The scouts promised to be very careful not to make a sound in following the guide, and so they dismounted to secure the horses and mules until their return from the beaver pond.

The scouts now had their first glimpse of these industrious little workers, that are found in large colonies everywhere throughout the Rocky Mountains. This particular colony had dug the canals from the pool to their pond, which was located in a bowl-like depression of the woods, and there dammed up the outlet. But few marauders passed here, and they lived in peace in their selected home-site.

There was a good growth of aspens all about the section, and these would supply food and lodgings for some time to come. The huts were erected in the middle of the largest pond of the chain. There were several beavers at work cutting the aspens when the party arrived on the edge of the pond, but so keen is the hearing and scent of these harmless animals, that they stopped work instantly, and slipped into the water, swimming unseen until they reached their huts.

"Huh! Dem 'fraid!" ejaculated Tally, with disgust on his face. "Come 'long—us see udder places."

Then he led through the aspen forest that fringed the pond, and reached the outlet where the dam had been constructed by the beavers. Here the scouts saw a shallow waterfall that fed another canal; this stream ended in another, but smaller, pond than the upper one they had first found. In this pond were a number of large huts, and many beavers at work at the farthest side of the pond.

"I believe they are building another dam, Tally!" exclaimed Mr. Gilroy, under his breath.

"Um—he am. Scout sit and watch."

So they all sat on the brink of the pond silently watching the busy workers as they cut down trees, dragged them into the water and then swam with them to the dam, where other beavers helped to place the heavy tree trunks in such a manner that any dead wood or débris floating downstream would catch and help to dam up the water.

"Why do they build another pond when there is such a big one above?" asked Betty.

Mr. Gilroy replied, "There is plenty of food for the family that now resides in the huts in the upper pond, but the colony is increasing so fast that they know there will not be room enough, or food enough, for all this winter. Hence they are building now, to provide ample shelter for the future. By starting another dam and thus creating a pond, these wise little woodsmen also secure an area of new aspens that will feed the new colony.

"Those canals that you see running out into the flat land beyond the new pond, are used as water courses to float the trees along into their pond. It is too bad we cannot see a beaver cut an aspen from that growth, and watch him float it until he brings it to its destination at the dam.

"But you can watch, from this vantage point, those old fellows at work. You see that big beaver that sits at one side of the two now cutting—well, he is the boss of that job. It is up to him to choose the best aspens for cutting and order his men to begin work, while he watches. Then when the tree is almost cut through he will warn them away, take up the work himself, and push on the severed trunk until it crashes down in the direction he wishes it to fall.

"You'll see how clever they are to have the aspen fall as near the water as possible, that they need waste no energy in dragging it over the ground to the pond."

The scouts watched, and sure enough! The old boss took up the work at a given signal to his two helpers to stand back, and soon after that, the aspen fell, half of it in the water. But the beavers must have heard a suspicious sound just as they were going to drag the tree across the pond, and they scuttled under the water.

Reluctantly the scouts turned away and went back to their horses, which they mounted, and soon they were riding along the way again.

"I never saw such enchanting flowers and gorgeous ferns!" exclaimed the Captain, enthusiastically.

"Um!" came from Tally, proudly, "him got more'n t'ousan' kin' flower in park!"

"Really! Oh, that we might secure one of each for a collection!" sighed Julie.

"It would take you longer than this summer to accomplish that," remarked Mr. Gilroy. "Here you will find some of the rarest orchids, as well as the hardiest kinds, known. Besides, you will find about fifteen species of gentian, the famous blue-fringed gentian among them. The largest columbines ever found grow here; and sweet peas in all conceivable shades of coloring. Not only can you add wonders to the botanical collections that you started in the Adirondacks, but you ought to be able to study many marvelous birds that nest in this primeval park."

So they rode along, stopping frequently to gather interesting flowers beside the trail, and to admire and watch the birds that could be seen everywhere.

"Jule, tell me about that bird swinging over your head"

It was during one of these short rests which had been caused by a crested bird of wonderful hue and unfamiliar form, that Joan and Julie, with a camera in hand, pushed a way through the bushes, the better to follow the bird's movements.

"Joan, you sit down there on that fallen pine and write down notes as I call them off, and I will climb up on top of that huge boulder and get a snapshot at him as he swings from that bough," said Julie, as she began climbing the rock mentioned.

Once she gained the top, she called back, "Of all the surprises! On the other side of this boulder is a steep descent that drops down to a dark pool.

Now who would ever have dreamed there was such a pool behind this rock!"

"Don't bother about pools or precipices now, Julie, but tell me about that bird, swinging right over your head. He'll fly away, if you don't 'make hay'!" laughed Joan, waiting with pencil suspended over the pad of paper.

The rest of the party had heard Julie's exclamation, and were urging their horses through the thick forest, nearer the two scouts. Tally jumped from his animal and came in the direction of the boulder, trying to catch a glimpse of the bird they were talking about.

"Jo, I really believe it is a young Rocky Mountain jay—the kind Gilly described to us. He is hopping into the higher branches now, and I can hardly see him," said Julie.

"Dear me, Julie! If only we could swear that we got a snapshot and description of the jay from actually watching him, what a fine thing it would be when we get home!" sighed Joan.

"Wait—I'll get out on the far end of this immense rock and try to get a full view of him," said Julie, moving across the top of the stone to the outer verge of it.

Suddenly the boulder began settling slowly down towards the pool. The soil underneath it had all been washed out by torrential rains, so that it barely hung in position when Julie climbed upon it. Now that she added her weight to its outer side, it began rolling—turning over and over in its heavy descent.

"Oh, oh! Save me, somebody! I'll be crushed to powder!" screamed Julie, who could not jump from that great height into the jungle, nor could she maintain a footing without doing the liveliest dance of her life.

It was well that the boulder was so heavy, and the pathway it rolled down so soft as to make it sink into the soil and grip a *digging* hold, as it turned and turned. Had the ground been rocky or the boulder smaller, it would have simply hurled itself into the water, carrying Julie with it.

Now, however, she danced and kept stepping like a trained circus animal does on a barrel to keep it rolling, while Joan cried fearfully, and Tally rushed through the bushes to gain the bottom of the gully. Julie had ceased screaming the moment she saw she was to be catapulted to an unforeseen doom, and now kept her wits about her to plan an escape.

She saw that the rock would settle down in the pool at about the same speed it took in rolling, and then she must be all prepared to spring off from its side, far out into the water, or be sucked underneath when it went down.

If the pool was shallow, she would be forced to slide off at the moment the boulder struck and would be left standing up in the water. She must wait to determine the best chance to take.

The time it took from the first starting of the rock down the grade to its striking the water was but a fraction of the time it takes to tell. Suddenly the huge boulder plunged into the quiet-looking pool, churning up the water to a froth, and instantly causing a "tidal wave" to raise the pool far beyond its customary water line and flow up the banks. The water, which had hitherto reflected every leaf and blade hanging over its surface, was so very deep that the monolith sank into its secret heart and was completely submerged.

As the rock sank, Julie sprang, taking her chances in striking something in the pool. But she escaped accident, and swam out of the whirling waters almost before the boulder had disappeared. Tally reached the pool as she jumped, and now flung himself in to help rescue her. She was equal to the test, however, and came up on land, dripping, but exultant and breathless from the dance and swim.

Tally helped her up the deep gully the rock had gouged out in its downward roll; and at the top where she had left Joan, there now stood waiting to embrace her, the entire party of riders. When all crying and hugging was ended, Julie laughed and said:

"Folks, give me a boulder-ride in the Rockies, every time, instead of an ordinary toboggan! Even snowshoes and skis are tame in comparison."

They laughed because they were so relieved at Julie's escape, but the Captain exchanged glances with Mr. Gilroy, and both shook their heads in despair of ever taming such a wild creature.

"In future, Julie, leave a Rocky Mountain jay where it hides, and study the colored prints shown in the bird book," advised Mr. Vernon, who had felt both for himself and his wife the severe nervous strain while the incident was being enacted.

"Oh, Uncle, half the fun of scouting in the Rockies comes from just these experiences. Just think of all we can talk about this winter, when we are hibernating at home!" exclaimed Julie, ready in spirit, at least, for another joy-ride.

They now resumed the trip that had been so unexpectedly interrupted, and came to an elevation in the trail. From this point they had a glorious view of the surrounding peaks in the park. Tally pointed out Long's Peak, which towered over their heads, and Mt. Meeker alongside it, which appeared almost as high. Mt. Washington and Storm Peak were so closely allied to the first two heights that they looked like four points of the one mountain.

Mr. Gilroy waved his hand to the northwest of Long's Peak, saying, "All that region is called Glacier Gorge, where we are bound for. There are concentrated the enormous gorges, cliffs, and other glaciated freaks caused by cataclysms that occurred aeons ago. In my opinion, there is no lake, waterfall, or other beauty of the Alps that can compare to this Glacier Gorge, and I have seen them all."

"If we are so near by, why can't we visit them all?" asked Joan.

Mrs. Vernon took fright, "*Never*—with the responsibility for you girls on my hands!"

"But, Verny, if we slip, we won't be on your *hands*,—it will be a glaciated scout on an ice-floe," laughed Julie.

Mr. Gilroy laughed. "And they'll be safer in glacier fields where they know there is great danger if they are careless, than beside quiet little pools, upon a rock that looks as solid as the planet itself."

Mrs. Vernon now turned beseeching eyes upon her husband. "Dear, you will persuade Gilly not to lead us into such places?"

"Oh, but Verny!" interpolated Julie. "Do let us go to see at least *one* glacier!"

"How can you, Julie! When *you* are the one always getting into trouble!" returned the Captain, wonderingly.

"Don't I always manage to get out of trouble again without causing any fatality—only amusement for the Troop?"

They all admitted that this was true, and finally the Captain was coaxed to listen to the argument in favor of visiting the glaciers.

"I haven't the slightest idea of riding past these glaciers and leaving Gilroy to explore them alone," remarked Mr. Vernon.

"If we agree to tie ourselves to your apron-strings, Verny, will you feel resigned to our going?" asked Julie, meekly.

"If five scouts dangle from my apron-strings, how can I scramble for myself?" laughed the Captain; but the girls knew she was weakening in her former refusal.

With wise looks exchanged between scouts and the two men, the subject was dropped for the time being. So they descended the height where they had obtained such a fine view of the peaks, and rode along the trail that was so heavily screened by forest trees as to cast a gloaming underneath them, even in the brightest sunshine.

"Gilly, how came these vast mountains here?" asked Judith.

"Yes, Gilly, why are they not scattered impartially over the land?" added one of the other scouts.

"While we are traveling along a good trail, let me tell you what I have gathered from scientific books on the subject," returned Mr. Gilroy.

"It is evident that the Rockies were the first points of land to lift a head above the sea of water when the American Continent was born. As often happens in the families of mankind, where the youngest-born embraces all the points of beauty and abilities that are manifested in individual allotments to all other members of the same family, so it is with Nature's mountain-children.

"The Rockies, being the youngest born of mountain ranges of the earth, inherited, as it were, the combined beauty and strength and characteristics that were the best in all the others. But there was no jealousy on the part of the older mountains of earth, and it is doubtful if any one of them even knew of this new-comer to the family group. Each had all it could do with its own affairs, in those by-gone cycles.

"Of Earth's large family of mountains, the first-born to lift a head from sleep on the bosom of the 'mighty waters' were the British Isles. They were not high or mighty in geography, but they were destined to raise the highest and mightiest race of people on earth.

"Then the Norseland awoke, and yawned so widely, that the pinnacles of its jagged shore-lines instantly molded themselves into barriers to protect the land from the inundation of the sea. Then while this awakening took place, the marvelous Antilles sat up from the cradle of the ocean and cried to Mother Nature to be lifted out of their bed. And Nature, who abhors a vacuum, gave her eager help to South America.

"Having given birth to these fine prominences, Nature seemed disinclined to cease from her creative activity. She believed it best to finish the allotted number of children, and then raise them all together. So the mountains of Labrador appeared, closely followed by the Atlantic Coast mountains.

"Then something happened in the bowels of the earth-planet that caused it to swallow so much salt-water from the seas that had covered its surface, that the great ranges of the Rockies stood up.

"Aeons passed during this great upheaval, and aeons more passed before islands dotted the 'face of the waters' and God said 'Let there be' and there was!

"It is said that the tremendous struggle in the womb of Mother Earth to give birth to the Rockies was Nature's hardest labor. As we gaze on the result of the mighty upheaval that has given us these wonderful mountains, does not your imagination paint 'cause and effect' better than mere words ever can?"

With many eager questions from the scouts, about cataclysms, glaciers, volcanoes, and other forces that helped build the dry land above the face of the seas, and with Mr. Gilroy's lucid and interesting descriptions of such work, the party reached the beautiful tract known as Estes Park.

"Here's where we camp for the night, Scouts,—unless you have something more important to do," announced Mr. Gilroy.

They laughed. "Now, Gilly! What more important date is there than to eat a good supper," added Anne.

The scouts teased her at that, but Mr. Vernon said, "I have an important date for those who will go with me."

He took up his fishing tackle, and instantly the scouts signified their eagerness to "keep the date" he had with the fish. Mr. Gilroy remained with Tally to look after camp arrangements and unload the mules. Then the horses and mules were turned out to pasture, while supper was prepared.

Because of the heavily wooded country they were to go through, Tally had not bothered to carry any tentpoles. It was an easy matter to run the ropes through the eyelets of the canvas, and string up the shelter to handy tree trunks. Hence the tents were up, and Mrs. Vernon was asked to weave the balsam beds upon the ground, inside them, before the girls returned.

Fuel was plentiful and a fire was soon burning, whereby supper could be cooked. Tally now began preparing his various dishes for the meal, while the Captain spread out the cloth on the grass for a table.

So excellent is the fishing in these forests, that the two camp-cooks had not had time to complete baking the bread-twist, or boil the potatoes, before the anglers arrived with a fine mess of fish. These were cleaned and placed in the large frying-pan where red and white streaked slices of bacon were crisping.

The savory odor that soon arose to mingle with the immediate surrounding air made every one sniff audibly, and wish supper was ready to eat. While the Captain added the finishing touches to the supper, she remarked to the scouts:

"I keep brushing so many little black insects from the cloth, and yet they seem to swarm about more than ever. Ask Tally what I can do to drive them away."

Mr. Gilroy overheard her, and replied, "I guess we are in for a plague of midges. No use trying to get rid of them by hand, and no use moving camp, as they infest the woods all about, when they do appear; and they last, sometimes, for several days, then they disappear as suddenly as they came."

As the scouts began to scratch at faces, necks, and limbs, Tally remarked, encouragingly: "De's not so badder."

"I hope you don't raise any worse pests than these in your Rockies!" cried Ruth, her hands and face red from irritation.

"Jus' wait. De'se meegies go wid sun, but moskeet—he come an' sing all night, an' bite all same."

In spite of the discomfort the little black imps caused, the scouts had to laugh at Tally's form of condolence. Evidently he, with his tough skin, preferred midges to songsters at night.

"Why should they swarm about now, when we never saw one on the way here?" asked Joan, in an aggrieved tone.

"It's going to rain, and that always drives them up from the underbrush and wet places where they live during the dry hours," explained Mr. Gilroy.

He had been occupied in crushing caribou leaves between his palms, and now the scouts turned to watch him. When he had extracted the juice from the leaves, he showed the girls how he rubbed it over his neck, face, and arms. This was very effective to keep away the pests for a time; but one had to keep on rubbing the fresh leaf-juice on the skin at intervals because the moisture evaporated with the heat from the body.

Supper—and it was a delicious one—over, Mr. Gilroy said to the guide, "Tally, we've got to make a smudge fire all right."

"Um!" agreed Tally, "see tent; him all cover wid bites."

The girls laughed at the Indian's graphic words, for the canvas was black with pests,—mosquitoes and black flies, as well as the midges.

Every available pan was requisitioned for use as braziers. And movable smokes, that Tally manufactured of pine shavings, smudged with damp material, effectively fumigated the camp and drove away most of the insects. But the scouts had to wave balsam fans quite vigorously to make the choking smoke that circled about them eddy away.

Tally arranged a chain of these smudge-fires about the camp ground, and provided elaborate means of keeping the pests away through the night. But all precautions were useless when the mean little mosquitoes got in between the open places in the canvas, and began their songs. Every one was healthily tired, though, and all the needlelike thrusts of the insects could not keep the girls awake.

In the morning, Julie said, "What should we have done if Tally had not smoked away millions of the creatures!"

And Joan said, "Why, infinitesimal atoms of Dandelion Troop would now be flying all over Estes Park to await Judgment Day!"

CHAPTER SIX
A MULE'S PLEASANTRIES

Long's Peak had been "done" to every one's satisfaction, and other neighboring peaks had been scaled. Estes Park was now becoming so familiar an environment that the scouts no longer thrilled at each new experience, but were eagerly looking forward to fresh excitement.

"Well, Tally, how about trekking northwards?" asked Mr. Gilroy of the guide, one night after supper.

"All 'leddy," returned the Indian.

"Frolic and Jolt seem to be deucedly gay after this long vacation," ventured Mr. Vernon, eyeing the frisky pack-mules.

"Um—Jolt him big kick," said Tally, signifying with a hand held above his head, how high the animal kicked that day.

"Our next lap of the journey will take all this freshness out of him, never fear!" laughed Mr. Gilroy.

That night while the scouts slept heavily, Tally heard a sound from the corral where he kept the horses and mules. He jumped up and ran over, but Jolt had broken his halter and had disappeared. He roused Mr. Gilroy and told him the news.

"Oh, let the old rascal go!" mumbled he, then turned over on his side and was fast asleep again. So Tally literally obeyed.

In the morning, however, Mr. Gilroy thought differently about his advice. Jolt was the best and strongest of the two mules, and the luggage of so many tourists was too much for Frolic, the smaller of the pack-animals.

Mr. Gilroy sighed heavily. "Well, the only thing to do is for all hands to turn out and hunt for Jolt."

"Why not have Verny and Betty, the two tender scouts of the troop, stay and strike camp?" asked Mr. Vernon. "We can go for the mule, while they pack everything and get ready for a start along the trail when we return."

In spite of the Captain's vehement declarations that she was not to be classed as too young or tender to enjoy a wild hunt for a fractious mule, the two were left behind, and the others started down the trail.

After many wanderings along side trails that offered temptations to such a wayward beast as Jolt, the hunters found him. Yes, Jolt was found, but it was another thing to catch him! After many vain attempts, Tally finally lassoed him, but the kicking, jumping animal seemed to think the more he performed the better the scouts liked it. After an absence of an hour, the captors filed back to camp, where Frolic—contrarily named—stood meekly waiting to be harnessed with the packs.

While Tally placed the two wooden crates on Frolic's back, Mr. Gilroy essayed to do the same with Jolt. But the mule had other intentions. The moment he felt the touch of the pack-frame he lit out with both hind legs. Poor Gilly not only caved in suddenly in the region under his belt, but he also sat down unceremoniously several paces behind Jolt.

"Um! Some bad Jolt!" declared Tally, scowling at the mule.

The opportune words were so amusing, that every one, Mr. Gilroy included, simply roared. But the Indian looked at them in silent wonderment. To his mind, these white men were *always* laughing.

Mr. Vernon now caught hold of Jolt's bit and held his head firmly between both hands, while Tally "hitched" the mule's feet so he could not kick or run again. Then the crates were strapped on and the packing began.

Jolt had the heaviest articles roped upon his packs. The canvas, blankets, and camping outfits were his portion. Frolic carried the duffel-bags and lighter baggage. Finally all were ready for the start.

The scouts got into the saddles, and Mr. Vernon followed suit. Tally and Mr. Gilroy were strapping the last leather around Frolic's packs. It was necessary to pull it in another hole to keep the pack from slipping under the beast's belly, but while Tally was so pulling it, Frolic gave a grunt. Another yank at the straps, and another louder grunt from Frolic made Betty interfere.

"I just know you are hurting poor Frolic dreadfully! She'll have a bad stomachache from those straps that are cutting her in half!"

Every one laughed at Betty's concern, but it drew attention to the work going on; and so, in watching Frolic being strapped up, every one forgot about Jolt. The old rascal saw his opportunity to escape to the delectable grazing ground from which he had been ruthlessly lassoed a short time before. So he wheeled and started for the trail.

But he forgot to make allowances for the projecting packs, and in passing between two tall pines with but a foot's space between the trunks, the crates became firmly wedged. So fast was he held, in fact, that Tally grinned when Julie yelled, "Jolt's running away again!"

Tally reassured her, "Jolt no run now—him rest awhile."

When Frolic had been made ready to start, the men went after Jolt. The aluminum cooking-ware had been hung, the last thing, upon the sides of the packs, and now the dishes were dented almost out of shape because they were the "bumpers" that came between the packs and the treetrunks. It took some time to dislodge the mule and his packs from between the trees, as it was necessary to protect the cooking utensils as much as possible.

This delicate operation was just being completed, when a cry from the scouts drew all attention back to Frolic again.

The tautly-drawn ropes caused Frolic an unpleasant sensation after the days of freedom from harness, so when she was left quite alone, she decided that rolling might ease matters. She lay down and rolled and kicked her heels high in the air, then she rolled again. She kept it up until the scouts knew that every bottle and box in their duffel-bags must be powdered into other necessities.

Tally rushed over and gave Frolic a vicious kick that instantly stopped her rolling, and caused her to lift inquiring eyes to those about her. Strange to say, Betty offered no protest when Tally kicked the mule again, to make her get upon her feet.

"There, now!" exclaimed Julie. "See that you maintain an upright behavior, you shiftless woman!"

The others laughed, for all were gay because the signal had been given to start along the trail. All went well after that, while the mules trotted closely after the horses, and the riders congratulated themselves that henceforth their troubles with the two mules were over. But they were to be undeceived further on.

They were descending a long rough hill when Jolt, who was the last beast but one in the line, heard a strange sound coming from his packs. Tally heard and recognized the metallic banging of some pans that had become loosened when the packs were wedged between the tree trunks at the top of the mountain. But Jolt was not as wise as Tally, and the more he shook himself, and sidled against the trees, the louder came that queer jangle. Then he managed to pass between two trees in order to brush off the objectionable thing, but that made the jangling still worse. So he became desperate.

About this time, Tally rode over to the place where Jolt was trying to crush the noisy thing from his pack, and attempted to use a lash to make the beast stop his stubbornness. But the tip end of the whip was all that caught the mule, and he suddenly jumped. That made all the other utensils shake loose and rattle. This was too much for the annoyed animal, and he started to gallop down the trail.

Warning shouts from Tally made the riders in front get out of the way; the guide then threw his lasso. But it caught upon a knob that had become loose and was projecting from the crate. Jolt flew onward, but the large object that had been roped, fell upon the ground with a dull thud.

To every one's shocked surprise, the lassoed article proved to be the only bag of flour they had at that time. The cotton container burst open with the fall, and flour dusted softly out upon the surrounding scenery.

"We can scoop most of it up and sift it," suggested Joan.

"But what is there to put it in?" demanded Julie.

"It's so precious—we mustn't lose an ounce of it," added the Captain.

"We'll each have to take one of our large clean handkerchiefs, and fill as much in them as they will hold. The ends can be tied together, and each will have to carry her own package," suggested Anne, who was worried lest a good meal be forfeited.

"That's the only way, I guess," agreed Mrs. Vernon; so each one filled a handkerchief, and the rest of the flour was then pinned in the bag and carefully placed in Mr. Gilroy's charge.

When the riders were on the trail again, there was no sight of Jolt anywhere. Where he had gone with the camp outfit was a question. But Tally worried not. He said laconically:

"Jolt wait nex' uphill."

When the scouts reached the bottom of the descent, they found a swiftly-running shallow stream crossing the trail. And in this, with both packs submerged, but with head safely held above the cooling water, Jolt was stretched out.

"There he would stay, I suppose, until he was sure the queer life that made the jangle on his back, was snuffed out," said Mr. Gilroy, chuckling at the mule's "horse-sense."

That day when they stopped to cook dinner, Tally was most careful to leave the pack-frames on the backs of the mules, as that would prevent fresh arguments when the time came to resume the trip.

Fish abounded everywhere,—in the streams, in the lakes, or in the wayside rivulets,—so that there was never a lack of such food. Nor did it need expert anglers to catch the fish. It seemed to the scouts that the poor things were only waiting eagerly to be caught.

Having selected the camp site, Tally suddenly stooped and examined some recently made tracks. "Bear ben here," said he.

"Oh, a real live bear?" cried Joan.

"Did you think a dead one made those tracks?" retorted Ruth.

"I wish we could see him," said Julie, and this wish was seconded by all the other girls.

"If you want a close acquaintance with him, just follow that track. Doubtless he is sitting behind a treetrunk this very minute, planning what to do with you after he has embraced you fondly," said Mrs. Vernon.

"If they follow bear tracks like they followed the calf's hoofprints, they'll sure find something at the end of the trail," teased Mr. Gilroy.

All that morning the sun had remained under a heavy pall of clouds, but noon brought forth its hot shining rays, and the long-reaching fingers seeming to edge the grey clouds with molten gold. During the afternoon the sun had shone fitfully, but towards evening it set in a gorgeous bath of color, the stormbanks that were piled up about it, adding a barbaric touch to the scene.

Flaunting streaks of gold and crimson shot here and there from back of the clouds; and these in turn seemed to reach out in a confused riot of dazzling purple, amber and copper-edged mountains that rose in majesty overhead.

All this wondrous coloring faded rapidly, however, and in a short time the somber gray of the clouds again predominated. Then a chill spread over everything.

"Him rain sure!" remarked Tally, holding a palm to the wind.

"When?" asked Mr. Gilroy.

"Mebbe bed-time—mebbe after night."

"Then we'd better prepare for it beforehand," suggested Mr. Vernon.

"Collect plenty of wood and spread the rubber sheets over it," said Mr. Gilroy. "We'll see that the tent ropes are well fastened to-night so the wind won't carry away any canvas."

Tally was right. Rain began to fall about nine o'clock. At first it came gently and unobtrusively, but soon it was driven in sheets by high winds.

It was well the guide had rolled great pine stumps to the fire, to keep the necessary fuel dry through the night. Although the scouts, rolled in their rubber covers, were unconscious of the elements that raged about and over them, Tally sat up feeding the fire that kept an area about the sleepers dry all night.

Now and then the demoniacal gale would root up a mighty pine, and with a s-s-split and a cr-r-r-rash it would thud down, breaking through all the younger timber. At such sounds, the girls would murmur sleepily, "Did you see any old trees near camp?"

Invariably the reply would be, "No—only little ones."

Then all would sleep again, relieved at such an assurance.

The camp presented a sorry appearance in the gray dawn. Everything was soaked, and the horses looked washed out. Even Jolt looked moister than when he rose out of the stream at the base of the mountain.

Later the sun glanced through dripping foliage and sent its warming beams into the stiffened joints of the campers. And when Tally had called them all to a good hot breakfast, life took on a more cheerful hue.

The tourists seldom followed the beaten trail that ran to Flat Top Mountain or to the Glaciers, because Mr. Gilroy secured better results in finding rock formations and glacial débris in going by the old Indian trails. And Tally knew these trails as well as the surveyor knows his line-maps.

Not long after the scouts had resumed their ride along one of the unfrequented trails, the party reached a mountaintop. The Leader turned her head and craned her neck in order to see what the object was that stood clearly outlined from a crag that hung over a dangerous gulch.

"A Rocky Mountain goat! I verily believe," said Mr. Gilroy.

"Oh, oh! That's what we want to see!" cried the girls.

"And I want to get a good picture of it," added the Captain.

"Now's your opportunity," returned her husband.

"But we are too far away to focus the camera."

"If the goat will wait, you might go over there," laughed Mr. Gilroy.

"Verny, we could ride across this plateau and manage to get a much better focus," suggested Julie.

"And there may be a whole herd feeding on the grass down in the glade between these cliffs," said Mr. Gilroy.

"Oh, let's go and see!" teased the scouts; so the horses were left with Tally, and their riders crept carefully across the grassy knolls and glades that hid from their view the ravine where they hoped to see the goats.

They were well rewarded for their trouble, too. Down in the green basin, under the crag where the ram kept guard for his sheep and ewes, grazed a large flock of Rocky Mountain goats. The scouts had a sight such as few tourists ever are blessed with, and Mrs. Vernon took a whole film of excellent snapshots,—all but one exposure, and that was left on the chance of an unusual sight.

While they stood watching the herd, a great ram was seen bounding recklessly along the edge of the cliff that formed the wall of the glade directly opposite the scouts. He nimbly jumped from ledge to ledge down this almost perpendicular wall, and soon reached the herd.

Then another ram, that first sighted by the riders, also started down, going where there seemed to be absolutely no foothold for him. He would spring from the ledge and, scarcely touching the side rock with his hoofs, land upon a bit of shelf, thence on down to another tiny ledge far beneath, and so on until he reached the glade.

The two rams now conveyed an alarm to the sheep, and forthwith they started up the perpendicular wall at the end of the glen, winding a way along one ledge after another where no visible foothold was seen with the naked eye. Yet *they* found one, for they climbed, and having reached the top of the wall, they disappeared.

"Oh, pshaw! I meant to snap the last exposure with that wonderful picture of the herd going up the wall," exclaimed Mrs. Vernon in evident disappointment.

"You're lucky to get the ones you did, Captain. These Rocky Mountain sheep are the wildest on earth, and seldom can man come near enough to get snapshots as you did to-day. The Peruvian goats and those in Arabia are agile and daring, but they do not compare with these goats for agility, and faith in their footsteps.

"When we go further North in the mountains, this scene we just witnessed will seem like child's play to the feats those goats will accomplish.

"The lambs are even more intrepid than the elders, and have not the slightest bit of fear of falling. Strangely enough, they seldom fall, and are hardly ever injured. It is said that the only risks they run are when they happen to jump in strange territory where the ledges and footholds are not understood."

As Mr. Gilroy finished his interesting description, Mr. Vernon added, "I've read that the injuries or death that come to these little athletes are due to their traveling in strange places and along unfamiliar trails, as you just mentioned. But in their own crags and mountain recesses, no hunter can ever trap them. They will jump, no matter from what height, and are always sure of a secure footing somewhere."

The scouts were so absorbed in listening that they had paid little attention to their own footsteps as they retraced their way to join Tally. Here and there were small pits almost hidden by the long slippery grass that grew on and hung over the edges.

Julie was about to draw every one's attention to a great bird that hovered overhead, when her foot slipped on such grass and, in trying to catch hold of something to waylay her descent into the shallow pit, she managed to lay hold of Mr. Gilroy's leg. In another moment, he was sliding down with her.

"Look pleasant!" warned the Captain, as she quickly snapped a picture on the last exposure of the roll, and then laughed merrily as she turned the knob that wound up the film securely.

When the two coasters managed to scramble out of the hollow, midst the laughter of all, Mrs. Vernon said, "I am glad now that my last picture will be one so fitting to be shown with the others of the Rocky Mountain Athletes."

A great ram came out opposite the scouts

CHAPTER SEVEN
TALLY AND OMNEY ENTERTAIN

While seeking for a likely spot where they could pitch camp that night, Mr. Vernon saw smoke ascending from the pines a short distance away. Fearing lest a fire had started in some way, Mr. Gilroy and he quickly sought for the place and came upon an old acquaintance. Mr. Lewis and his guide, Omney, to say nothing of their Irish terrier, Scrub, were in camp, eating supper.

It was a pleasant surprise for both Mr. Lewis and Mr. Gilroy, as the two geologists had not met since their trip in the mountains many years before. So both parties soon joined camps and enjoyed themselves immensely.

After supper that night, the girl scouts heard of many wonderful experiences these friends had shared—the jaunts and jeopardies that always provide such thrilling stories after they are over. Finally Mr. Lewis remarked, "I came here this summer to hunt out a few of those glacial specimens we missed the last time, Gilroy."

"Now, that's strange, Lewis, because that is why I am here. Dr. Hayden mentions some in his latest book, and Tyndall Glacier is the only place I've ever heard of where there is any such moraine," said Mr. Gilroy.

"Have you been there, yet?" asked Mr. Lewis.

"No, 'but I'm on my way,'" laughed the scientist.

"Then take me with you, old pal! How about the rest of your party," said Mr. Lewis.

"Oh, Mr. Vernon is fast becoming as infatuated with the hunt for specimens as you or I ever were. So we'll share fifty-fifty if we can find anything worthwhile."

"And the ladies?" added Mr. Lewis.

"As they are tried and trusty scouts, they are fit for any trial of courage or endurance—is that enough?"

"That's a splendid recommendation for any one, Gilroy, but have you told them that exploring these glaciers is not as easy as sitting beside a fire and talking of the thrills?"

"I have no idea of dragging them down through the moraines with us; but they can accompany us on the trail and enjoy the camp while we wander about in our hunting. The guides can plan the girls' recreation for the time we are absent. Now, how does that strike every one?" said Mr. Gilroy.

Of course, every one agreed that the plan was great, so they rode forward in the morning, bound for the district around Tyndall Glacier. When they found a place that would make a comfortable camp for the time, the Indians went to work to arrange things for a week, or more, according to the geologists' plans.

Camp was pitched upon a knoll with plenty of pine trees so standing that natural tentpoles were readymade. The rain would drain from all sides of the knoll, and at one side ran a stream of pure spring-water. From the front of this campsite one could see the cold forbidding peak of Tyndall Glacier.

Mr. Lewis's guide, whose baptismal name was as difficult to pronounce as Tally's, was called Omney,—that being a good imitation of what it really was. Julie, who was always doing something funny, named him "Hominy."

As soon as the campsite had been decided upon, the two guides told the scouts to clear away all excrescences from the ground. This meant they had to take axes and cut out all brush and roots that would interfere with comfortable walking about. Then the girls said the place was as clean as a whistle, and Tally went over it carefully. But it was amazing how many "stick-up" obstacles he found, where everything had seemed so smooth.

While Tally was doing this, Omney supervised the cooking of supper, and soon various savory odors greeted the nostrils of the hungry scouts. Every one was ready to eat when Omney announced that it was ready, and then there was a period of silence for a time.

Supper was over with the sunset, and the long purpling shadows of the mountains crept up while the guides placed fresh fuel on the fire and sat down to smoke their pipes. The Rocky Mountain wilderness, untamed as yet, closed in about the group that sat around the fire, while certain unfamiliar sounds of wildlife in the forest reached the ears of the scouts; but they cared not for prowling creatures there and then, because the campfire provided ample protection.

The two Indians, not having seen each other since their masters' last trip, were in high feather; and when Mr. Gilroy suggested that they entertain the party, they quickly responded. Omney first chanted his tribe's Medicine Song; but before he sang he made obeisance to the four winds of heaven,—the North, East, South, and West,—that neither wind should forget Him who held them in the palms of His hands. He then explained that this honor and the song to follow were the opening forms to their daily worship of the Great Spirit.

He began in a deep-toned rhythmical chant, and he proceeded with the syncopated melody, now and then sifting in some queer sounds that *may* have been words, while he kept time with hands and feet. Finally this motion seemed to become an obsession, and he accompanied his sudden cries and exclamations with muscular actions and twists of his supple limbs. When he reached this point in the Medicine Song, Tally caught up a pan, and with muffled sticks beat time to the singing.

After a period of this weird performance, Omney began to circle the fire; Tally springing up, followed him in the dance. Their bodies doubled, turned, and twisted about, as if controlled by galvanic batteries. Their sharp ejaculations and hisses, interspersed in the singing, gave a colorful effect impossible to describe.

Suddenly, as if arrested by a shock, both Indians stood erect and perfectly still. They turned as if on pivots to glance upward, and saluted the four winds of heaven; then walked slowly over and sat down. Their performance was ended.

The encore they received was acknowledged with dignified smiles, but Omney made no sign to repeat his act. Then Tally stood up and bowed. He caught up a blanket that covered a balsam bed near by, and wrapped it about his erect form. He walked to the center of the camp circle and made a graceful acknowledgment for both entertainers; then he began to speak in a softly modulated voice, and with gestures that would have created envy in the best elocutionist, fascinating to any one who knew him as the quiet and unobtrusive guide.

"Brothers, I tell you the tale of the Blackfeet Tribe, how Thunder won his bride, and lost her again.

"In the long ago, when the Sky-People used to visit the Earth-Folk frequently, to demand pelts and other good things from the Earth Children in return for sparing their camps from the destructive lightnings and floods, three young maidens went to the woods to dig herbs.

"One of these three was the loveliest maiden to be found for many a league, and many a Brave had tried to win her affections. But she was fond only of her old father, Lame Bull.

"While Mink Maiden and her two companions were placing their herbs in bundles to carry back to camp, a dark thundercloud swept over the place, and passed on. However, it seemed as if venting its fury on the camp where the maidens lived.

"Then fell Mink Maiden upon her knees and promised Thunder Chief, saying, 'Spare my father and I will obey you in any way you may desire.'

"Thunder laughed, for that was exactly what he had hoped for. He instantly withdrew his storm from over the terrified village, and came close to the maiden who had made the rash promise.

"'I shall come for you soon, Mink Maiden, to ask you to keep your word.' With these words, Thunder flew away to the sky and disappeared through a hole.

"Soon again, the three maidens went to the woods for herbs and while two of them stopped to dig some roots, Mink Maiden went on alone. She saw a plant, rare and greatly desired by Lame Bull, and she pushed a way through the bushes to dig up the root. But when she reached the spot where it had been, she saw nothing.

"Suddenly, without sound or other sign, a handsome young chief stood where the plant had been. Mink Maiden was surprised, but when he spoke, saying, 'I am waiting for you to be my bride—will you come with me?' the maiden knew him.

"'I am Thunder Chief, and am come to have you redeem your vow.'

"Mink Maiden saw that he was tall and handsome, and naturally brave. He smiled so kindly that she knew he was gentle. But she coyly asked, 'What must I do to keep my word with you?'

"'Be my wife. Come with me to reign over the Sky People, for I am their Chief.' As he spoke he held forth his hands, and Mink Maiden placed her own confidently within his.

"He enfolded her closely in his cloak of winds, and springing up from the ground, carried her through the hole in the sky.

"When the two companions of Mink Maiden sought for her, she was not to be found anywhere. They ran to Lame Bull's lodge to tell him of her disappearance, and the entire village turned out to seek her. Everywhere they sought her, for she was beloved by young and old alike, but she was not found nor did they hear what had happened to her.

"Then came a stranger to that village and asked for Lame Bull's lodge. He was Medicine Crow Man, who had long desired Mink Maiden for a wife.

He had heard of her disappearance and by making strong medicine had learned where she was.

"After telling Lame Bull how he loved his daughter, and that he had power to find her, the old father promised that should Crow Man but find where she was, he should have Mink Maiden for a wife when she returned home.

"Crow Man then caught a blackbird and poured oil of black magic on his tail feathers. The bird was sent up into the sky to find if the lost maiden could be enticed to come back home. After several days the blackbird returned to Crow Man.

"'I could not fly through the hole in the sky, as the people have been ordered to close it with a great plant-root. But I sat on the under part of the roots and heard what was said. And this is it:

"'Thunder Chief carried Mink Maiden away to be his wife. He commanded that the hole be sealed, that his bride might not see through it and be tempted to return to her home. I heard say that she is very happy with Thunder Chief, and never thinks of those she left on earth.'

"'Very good, Blackbird, and for this news your tail feathers shall always shine as if with oil. But your curiosity and love for gossip must remain part of your weaknesses,' said Crow Man.

"He then went to Lame Bull and told all that he had learned through the blackbird. Then the villagers began to mourn Mink Maiden as one lost to them, for they never expected to see her again. But Crow Man determined to use every art in his power until she should come back.

"Time went by and the maiden was contented with Thunder Chief, and never remembered her earth people, for the root choked up the hole in the sky where memory might slip through.

"But one day she saw some people bring home herbs and roots which they had dug for the Chief. Mink Maiden asked them where they found them as she, too, wished to dig some. They told her where to go for them, and with basket on her arm she went forth.

"It happened that it was the summertime, when Thunder Chief had to be away many times, fighting the earth people with storms, so she wandered away alone from the lodge where she lived with her husband.

"She sought eagerly for the plant she wanted, until she finally came to the great root that blocked the hole in the sky. This she thought must be the place where the other women dug, and she forthwith began to dig also.

When she had dug deeply, she pulled on the root, and up it came, leaving a great hole where it had been.

"Mink Maiden was amazed at the size of the root, and leaning over, gazed into the hole, and far down saw the earth. At the same time a blackbird flew quite near the hole, and said, 'Mink Maiden, your father cries for you to come home.'

"Then memory returned to the maiden, and she remembered her people. When Thunder Chief returned from his battles, he found his beloved wife in tears. She cried that she wished to visit her own people on earth. And so, after useless pleadings with her, the husband agreed to take her home for a visit.

"Accordingly, he flew with her to Lame Bull's lodge and left her to visit her father. She looked well and comely, and the old Chief was overjoyed to see his child again. When she told how happy she was with Thunder Chief, the father sighed.

"'I had hoped you would choose to live on earth where I could visit you. Crow Man loves you, and has been here many times to ask for you.' Lame Bull then told of the promise he had made Crow Man.

"But the Mink Maiden laughed, saying, 'I am married to Thunder Chief, so Crow Man cannot have me.'

"In a short time after this, Thunder Chief came for his wife, and asked Lame Bull to forgive him for carrying away his only child. Then Lame Bull said, 'Allow her to remain yet a short time.'

"Thunder Chief presented his father-in-law with a Medicine pipe, and taught him to sing the Sky Song that would always protect his tribe from storms and destruction from lightning. Then he turned to his wife and bade her good-by for a time, adding, 'I will return soon for you, so be ready to go home. You shall visit your father often after this.'

"He then flew away and Mink Maiden sat with her father for several days, waiting for her husband to come. But there had been a dreadful commotion in the sky the day after he flew away from the village, and the people said they had never seen such blinding lights and such terrific rumbles, so the wife knew her husband was having a great battle with some one.

"The cause was, Crow Man had fought with Thunder Chief, although Mink Maiden never knew that. Crow Man was subdued for that time, but in the fall he sent the blackbird northward to call out all the Arctic forces to come and help keep Thunder Chief from coming to earth to carry back his wife. And so they did.

"Crow Man called often at Lame Bull's lodge and all through the winter, when Mink Maiden sighed because her husband came not, Crow Man felt happy and tried to make her believe Thunder Chief had forgotten her.

"Then spring came on, and Mink Maiden wondered still more because she heard nothing of her husband, nor came he to the lodge. Crow Man urged his suit, but she laughed, for she was a wife already, she told him.

"All through that second year she sat in her father's lodge and waited; but not a word heard she from the Sky People, nor did Thunder Chief come for her, although she was told that he had been heard of in other parts of the country, so it was learned that he was alive and active. Strange to say, neither Mink Maiden nor Lame Bull remembered the Medicine that had been given the old Chief, to keep away all storms from the tribe. This had proved so effectual that Thunder Chief could not communicate with his wife because of it, and she never went beyond the village limits, where he might have met her.

"That winter Crow Man urged his love again, and begged Mink Maiden to marry him, so she finally sighed and said:

"'I am Thunder Chief's wife, but if he does not come to claim me in another year, I will go with you.'

"Crow Man was overjoyed at hearing this, and he worked very hard to keep away all reports of Thunder Chief from the village. Then, as Mink Maiden waited hopelessly for the return of her husband, the year rolled by and Crow Man came for her. So she followed him to his lodge, although she still remembered Thunder Chief with regret.

"Crow Man was jealous of her memories and was determined to cure her. So he planned a dreadful thing. He sent the blackbird for the North Forces, and when they came in obedience to his order, he told them what they must do.

"Then he asked Mink Maiden to walk with him through the lovely woods a distance from the village. And as they walked, the wife saw Thunder Chief approach with outstretched arms and call to her in a yearning voice. He cried, 'At last, my beloved, you are where I can reach you. All these moons have I longed to meet you, but you sat in the lodge where my own Medicine that I gave your father, kept me away.'

"Thunder Chief hurried forward, but the Arctic Forces ran out from their hiding-places and fell upon Thunder Chief, just as he was waiting to enfold his beloved in his cloak. With their cold icy blasts and whirling snow and sleet, they overpowered poor Thunder Chief. In spite of his roaring and sharp lightnings, his power was frozen into sharp points. And that is how icicles came to be upon all Nature's trees and bushes when the North Forces scatter broadcast the power of the Sky Forces.

"Mink Maiden saw her beloved turned to ice before her eyes, and she went away, weeping, to her home with Lame Bull. And Crow Man besought her in vain to return to his lodge. She would not, and that is why the Crow always calls, 'Come, come, come!'

"And every year when the time returns that Thunder Chief came for his bride and the North Forces overpowered him, you will see Mink Maiden come from the woods, weeping over her lost love."

When Tally concluded this legend, the scouts called for another, but Mr. Gilroy mentioned that the three men planned to get an early start for the glacier fields and it was time to retire. So the two guides prepared the fire for the night and the girls began their good-nights.

Mr. Lewis stopped them, however. "Scouts, I want to say a word to you. I notice that you do not know the Indian walk—the only way to walk in the woods and not grow weary. In fact, the way all the wild creatures walk, whether they run or creep, without making a sound that will attract attention to them."

"No one ever gave it a thought, Lewis," admitted Mr. Gilroy. "Now that you mention it, suppose you show the girls, and let them practice, to-morrow, with the guides to teach them."

Mr. Lewis then demonstrated the white man's walk and the natural gait of the Indian. The two guides walked to show exactly what he meant, and then the girls were told to do it.

"Walk perfectly erect,—not leaning from the waist-line forward, as most people do. Plant your feet with more weight coming upon the sole instead of on the heel of the foot. Always turn your toes straight forward, and take your steps, one foot directly in front of the other so that the track you leave will look like a one-footed man walking a chalk-line.

"Once you have acquired this gait, you will wonder that you ever walked in any other manner. You can walk a narrow ledge, or stick to any foothold that a living creature can go on, without slipping from lack of room for your feet.

"But the greatest benefit such a walk is for one in the forests, is that you can proceed without making any noise. You will not be soaked with the dew that remains on leaves or undergrowth; and after you have taken a long hike you will feel fresh, and have enough energy to start on another trip."

The scouts practiced that night, and had many a good laugh at the awkward steps they took when first trying the Indian gait. But they finally acquired it, and with daily practice in the woods, they soon walked as well as Mr. Lewis himself.

CHAPTER EIGHT
SCRUB'S UNEXPECTED HUNTING TRIP

Mr. Lewis's dog, Scrub, was a never-ending source of fun and entertainment for the scouts. He was a most intelligent animal, and understood everything said to him. In fact, his owner said that Scrub was far more intelligent and practical than many human beings he had known. He also told the girls that they could follow Scrub into the woods if the guides could not go with them, and he would always bring them back by easy trails—he had such a wonderful sense of location and traveling.

The first day in camp, after the three men had started for the glacier field, Tally and Omney had to complete minor details in the camping arrangements, so the scouts did not ask to be taken for a hike up the mountainside. Scrub nosed about for a time, trying to attract the girls' attention by his "talk" but when they failed to understand, he ran away alone, and was not seen again until late that afternoon.

He came tearing into camp, barking excitedly, and jumping about the guides and the scouts, as if to tell them of some thrilling adventure he had experienced in the woods that day. They made much of him, but finally his master scolded him for barking so shrilly, so Scrub placed his stub tail between his hind legs and crept under a tree.

The next day Scrub began again to caper about and bark excitedly to invite the scouts to go hunting with him. But they laughed, and Julie said to him, "We're going with Tally and Hominy after a while."

It was not, however, to Scrub's liking that they tarried so long in camp, and he started away alone. Then when the guides were all ready to go with the scouts, the dog was not to be found.

"Ev'buddy take gun dis time," suggested Tally.

"Oh, what fun! Shall we find any wild animals?" asked Joan.

"Mebbe—dunno."

The Captain warned the girls about using the rifles without first noting all the conditions, and told them not to use them under any circumstances if there was no danger. As each scout knew perfectly well how to carry the firearm so as to protect others, and as every one used precaution at all times, there was no risk of accident.

The woods were still wet from the heavy night-dew, but the girls found their newly-acquired step protected their skirts from much moisture. The sun was sending its searching light into every secret nook of the forest, and soon the dew evaporated and the gloom in the dense woods brightened. The many hitherto hidden things in the forest now stood clearly revealed in the sunshine.

They followed the trail that led up the mountainside back of the camp. Tally waved his hand in an inclusive sweep at the sun, then at the forest it shone upon, and remarked, "Him no shine in long. Onny mornin'—den shadow come back an' fores' grow black agin."

The scouts were eagerly gazing at one thing or another in their progress up the steep trail when Betty gave a little cry and jumped out of the way.

"What is it—a rattler?" cried many voices, anxiously.

"No, but the cutest little rabbit I ever saw,—just like the one Verny caught and helped in the Adirondacks, you know."

Tally then added, "No rattlers on dis side Rockies, all on udder side mountains."

"Betty's scream would make one think she was facing a grizzly!" said Julie, scornfully.

"I wasn't frightened,—it startled me, that's all," Betty said, defensively.

"Was it big enough for rabbit pie?" asked Anne, unwittingly calling down the reproaches of all the scouts upon her head.

As they scolded Anne for always thinking of something to eat,—even a darling little rabbit,—Tally suddenly held up a hand for silence. Instantly everything was quiet. Then they heard distinctly the plaintive cry of a distressed animal.

"Dat deer call. Him 'fraid an' need help. Shall us go?" explained Tally.

"Oh, yes, Tally, by all means!" exclaimed Mrs. Vernon.

So they pushed a way through the thick screen of pines until they came to a clearing where the trees had been burned down. The sun shone into the place, clearly showing the scene of a forest tragedy which was about to be enacted there.

The two guides made way for the scouts to crowd up beside them, and there they saw a well-grown deer in the center of the tiny park. It was still young and inexperienced, as was shown by the way it backed around and voiced its horror and fear.

"What is it afraid of, Tally?" questioned the Captain, because her unaccustomed eyes saw nothing to fear.

"See on limb dere—where deer must go if she like to get out?" whispered Tally, pointing to one end of the clearing where a giant pine spread its branches far over the place.

Along the lowest bough crouched a panther, ready to leap. Its green eyes gleamed with hungry desire for the choice breakfast so near, and its sinuous tail whipped gracefully back and forth against the tree. But its gaze wavered from the deer to something at the other end of the clearing. What could be restraining this ferocious beast, whose claws, as they dug sharp nails into the wood of the tree, appeared ready to rip open the tender flesh of its prey?

Two sides of the clearing were made impassable for the deer by the close growth of aspens, interlocked like a brush-fence. At one end of the clearing the panther kept guard, but what was the cause of the starting eyes of the deer as it gazed at the nearer end—the end where the scouts stood?

"Ah, Omney—see?" breathed Tally, softly, as he pointed.

Then they saw a grey-brown animal about the size of Scrub, with a stubby tail. Its body was thick and short, and its head was round. It had gleaming eyes, green-slitted like a cat's. Its ears were sharp-pointed and stood erect. The mouth was partly open, with the tongue showing its red edge between the fanglike teeth. Its rusty color merged so perfectly with the bushes that it was small wonder the scouts had not seen it immediately.

Its expression, the crouching pose, its tense muscles—all denoted its eagerness to taste the blood of the deer, but there was the panther to reckon with first! Now the girls realized the danger of the young deer. How could the poor thing hope to escape from a panther and a lynx?

When the lynx sensed the human beings, she snarled viciously, but showed no fear. Her entire attention was given to the movements of the panther. But the fact that her natural enemies, human beings, stood so close to her, made her act sooner than she might have done.

Tally whispered the situation in a breath. "Pant'er no jump, fear lynx get him an' en get deer. Lynx 'fraid to jump firs' 'cause pant'er den jump on bof an' eat 'em."

Then Omney whispered, "Tally shoot pant'er, an' me shoot lynx—same time. When I say fire—den shoot!"

So the two guides slowly lifted their rifles and aimed. But the lynx had crept closer to the deer, which in turn sent a swift look of apprehension back at the beast that was now preparing to spring the moment the lynx leaped. The deer lifted its muzzle high and bleated forth a wailing cry, and at the same moment two rifles sounded.

The instant before they rang out, the lynx had jumped right at the throat of the deer, and the instant after the panther had leaped also. The bullet sped faster than the lynx could spring, and the latter fell with a heavy thud to roll over in the buffalo grass at the forefeet of the deer.

Omney's shot at the panther, however, struck its right shoulder instead of a fatal spot. When the lynx rolled under the nose of the panic-stricken deer, the poor creature jumped over against the wall of aspens, and this leap spared its life. For the panther, instead of ripping open its throat as it planned to do, clawed a tear in its side and then rolled over on the grass. Instantly, the wild beast was up and about to spring again, when a shot from Tally's gun ended its preying.

The frightened deer had seen the animal rise to spring again, but her eyes were so blinded with the pain and fury of the gash in her side, that she leaped high and brought both hoofs down upon her dead antagonist. Again and again she lifted her stiffened forelegs and drove her sharp hoofs into the spine of the dead panther. Finally, however, the deer realized that her enemy was dead, and swiftly she wheeled and fled from the clearing through the opening opposite the scouts.

As she disappeared, the girls relaxed the nervous tension that had held them absolutely motionless during the battle. Now they sighed, and Mrs. Vernon sat down where she had stood. Betty began crying softly, and said, "The poor deer! I hope its side will heal."

"Sure! Him go roll in mud of shallow spring and it heal," Tally assured her.

The lynx and panther were found to be splendid specimens of their individual kinds, and the scouts had the satisfaction of knowing that this big game had not been shot for mere sport. But, having saved the deer's life by shooting the two wild beasts, the pelts naturally became trophies for the scouts to send home.

"They're awfully big brutes, girls. We'll never be able to carry them both back to camp to-day," said Mrs. Vernon.

"Skin 'em—onny take back pelts," said Omney.

"We want to have them stuffed, Hominy, so we need the heads and feet, too," said Julie.

Tally looked at Omney and spoke in his native language. Then he turned to the scouts and interpreted what he said.

"I say, Omney skin animals wid head an' feet on—us go on an' help Omney on way back. Him done skin den."

As no new adventure befell them that day, they retraced their steps and stopped for Omney and the pelts. That night the story was told to the three men, and it lost none of its coloring by having five scouts tell it, turn and turn about.

Scrub did not return to camp that night, and Mr. Lewis told Omney to start immediately after breakfast in the morning and see if any untoward accident had happened to the dog. Tally and the scouts would not remain behind, for they were very fond of the pet and worried lest he had been killed by a wild beast.

They chose the trail they had seen Scrub take the two previous days, and after climbing the mountain for a time, Tally and Omney argued over following a faint trail through a jungle. Tally pointed to a paw-track in the soft earth, but Omney declared it was not a dog's track.

Yet Tally won his way, and started into the dense thicket. He had not gone more than a few yards before he exclaimed jubilantly and pointed to a wisp of Scrub's hair that had been caught on a briar. Then Omney meekly admitted that Tally must be right in his intuitions.

After following the faint trail for a short time, Julie called out, "I'm sure I heard a dog bark just now."

"Let's shout. Maybe Scrub's lost and is calling to us," explained Betty, anxiously.

"Lost! Now Betty, you don't know that dog if you say he could be lost," retorted Joan.

They all distinctly heard a shrill bark, now, and Tally said, "Sound like him got wild animal trapped, an' wan' us help."

Finally they were near enough to hear Scrub bark and yelp in reply to the plaintive whining of some other animal. Then Tally advised the girls, "You no call Scrub when you come up. Dog look to see you, an' animal jump on him. No say anyting, but wait an' let Tally shoot."

This was hard sense, and the scouts agreed to obey. Just then they reached a spot where the forest trees were not so closely grown. Tally held his rifle ready to shoot if necessary, to spare the dog's life, but when he came out of the fringe of pines that circled the small clearing where the dog barked, he stood amazed.

The scouts deplored the fact that the camera had been left at camp, as usual, for here was a most unique picture. Scrub stood stiffly, the hair along his spine standing upright from excitement. His stub tail vibrated so swiftly that one could not see it move—it seemed a blur of action. His front legs were braced, and he was yelping and barking at two little bear cubs.

They appeared as distressed and confused as the dog. One, the larger of the two, glared at Scrub with ferocious mien and at intervals, when the dog stopped barking for time to breathe, it would charge threateningly, but never got near enough to grapple with the dog.

The smaller cub circled whiningly about a huddled mass that lay under a great pine log. It would sniff about the heap and then sit upon its little haunches and cry quiveringly. It was this wail the scouts had heard in the distance.

At times Scrub would run over to the trail whence he found his friends approaching, then the little male-cub would join his sister at the black heap, and both would whine pitifully to the mother that was insensible to their cry. The moment Scrub was aware of any movement on the part of his opponent, he would tear back to engage his enemy in another wrangle of sounds.

"Um! No wonder Scrub no come home las' night!" laughed Tally.

"Maybe that's why he was so excited the night before—he wanted to tell us," ventured Joan.

"Yes, but I'm surprised that he remained, when he found we would not follow him," added Julie.

"He may have feared we might move camp and he would be left behind," suggested Mrs. Vernon.

"I go see why mudder don' help cubs," said Tally. So he started across the clearing, followed by the girls.

"Um! See—big log fall from tree jus' when bear go un'ner," said the Indian, pointing up at the split bough that had been severed by lightning, with its heavy end left dangling for a time. It had fallen and struck the black mother-bear just as she was passing under, and it must have instantly killed her.

"The poor little babies!" sighed Betty.

"Can't we catch them and train them?" asked Julie, eagerly.

"Dem die sure in woods—or beastes eat 'em," said Tally.

"Dear me, we mustn't have that!" cried Mrs. Vernon.

"If we could only tame them and send them to the Zoo in New York—what a fine thing that would be for the Girl Scouts' Organization. It would be quite an honor," exclaimed Ruth.

During the unfamiliar sound and sight of the scouts, the cubs blinked fearfully at them. What new calamity was now at hand—and mother lying there so still and helpless?

Scrub was ordered away from the bears and made to mind, while Tally planned how to catch the cubs.

"I use rope an' lasso bof," said he.

"We'll surround the cubs, Tally, and Scrub can keep guard so they won't run away, while you catch them," planned Julie.

It was an easy task to catch the little girl-cub and tie her to a tree near the mother bear. But it was another matter to catch the boy-cub. Tally threw the lasso, but it merely struck the rump of the little fellow as he turned to investigate what his sister, who had been given a chunk of cake by one of the scouts, was eating.

The cub resented the slap from the rope, and snapped at it. But Tally dragged the lasso back, coaxing the bear-cub much nearer. When the rope was caught up to coil again, the frightened little fellow raced back to the tree where his sister sat. He was so cunning in his awkward gait that the scouts laughed heartily.

This time the rope caught him truly, and he rolled over with a jerk. He clawed and snapped and yelped at the bonds that kept him from running away; and when Tally took in the rope, the cub snapped viciously at him. Then the guide had to throw his coat over the cub's head and fall upon it to wrap him in the folds.

But the forepaws were free, so the cub used them well, trying to tear the garment away from his head. So strong was the little fellow that Tally had his hands full to finally tie him about the neck. In this fight the cub earned his name of "Snap."

When both cubs were securely tied to the tree, Tally went over to examine the old mother-bear. The scouts followed and stood looking down upon the huge body sprawled under the heavy log.

"Her dead at once. Her not hear babies cry—or nuddin'," explained Tally, trying to lift the log from her back.

Several of the scouts assisted and soon the tree bough was rolled away, Scrub managing to get in every one's way during the procedure.

"Her dead mos' two day—babies no get milk to eat," said Tally, after examining the teats and body of the bear.

"Mebbe we coax home wid eats," suggested he, as he glanced from mother to cubs and back again.

"Tally, I brought some candy in my pocket," said Anne, instantly producing the sweets.

"Bear like sugar. Us lead cubs easy wid dis."

"Tally, how can we keep this dead bear so we can have her skin, too," now asked Julie, anxiously.

"Oh, if we could only ship home such a magnificent bear pelt, wouldn't we be proud!" sighed Joan.

"Kin skin and bury 'um now. Come back mornin' an' carry to camp. Got han' full wid two cub to-day," grinned the Indian.

"Oh, if you boys would skin it and save it for us!" sighed several eager scouts.

So the guides sharpened their great knives that they always carried in their belts, and began work on the dead bear. The girls would have fainted at such a sight a year before, but now they stood by without a quiver and watched the Indians skin the animal.

The pelt was soon stripped from the carcass, and the former was buried deep under the log, while the latter was left for the wolves, or other animals. While Tally finished this work the scouts gathered berries to feed to the starved cubs. The latter were so famished that they eagerly ate everything given them.

All the way home the scouts took turns in holding bits of candy in front of the cubs' noses, to make them run for it. At some of these "home-runs" the cubs got the best of it, and the scouts had to drop the candy and jump aside, or be clawed in the bears' eagerness to get the sweets. At such times Scrub barked and jumped at the harnessed cubs, and they in turn would fight back, so there ensued a wild scene of battle until Tally got the upper hand again.

Once the cubs were in camp and caged they became tame and friendly with every one,—even Scrub failed to draw a snarl from Snap now. The smaller of the two bears was named Yap, as she was forever wanting something to eat and yapped when she could not get it.

In a few days' time they were freed from the homemade cage and tethered to a tree during the daytime. They furnished great amusement for the scouts; and Scrub was peeved because every one showed so much attention to these horrid little brutes, while *he* would permit petting without a snap if his friends were so inclined.

The campers had been on this site for almost two weeks before the men mentioned that they were ready to move along. The cubs were quite tame now, and ran about camp, playing with every one who would play with them. They were fine and plump, and the scouts gave much time to the currying of their soft silky coats and to teaching them tricks.

"What do you scouts intend doing with Snap and Yap when we start on the trail again?" asked Mr. Gilroy.

"Where do you plan to go from here, Gilly?" asked Julie.

"Why, Lewis is going back now that he has secured the special specimens he came to the glaciers for," returned Mr. Gilroy; "but we are to go along to Flat Top, where I hope to spend some time at Tyndall, you know."

"You told me, Gill, that you wanted to visit Mills' Moraine and hunt for glacial deposits there," ventured Mr. Lewis.

"So I did, but it is simply impossible for me to lead the scouts such a dance, and now that they have two bears to dance along with them, I shall have to forego Mills'," laughed Mr. Gilroy, longingly.

"Is Mr. Lewis going right back to Denver, did you say?" asked Julie.

"Yes, he has a public lecture to give at the Auditorium, so he cannot go on with us," explained Mr. Vernon.

"Then listen to my idea, and tell me what you think of it—everybody," exclaimed Julie, eagerly.

"Why can't Mr. Lewis take back our pelts and the cubs, and express them home for us?"

The very audacity of the suggestion made every one laugh at first, but after much talking it seemed not so impossible.

"Then Gilly and Uncle can go through their wonderful heaps of glacial débris, while Tally guides us along the trail to the Flat Top. We will meet again at the foot of Tyndall Glacier," said Julie.

So out of all the talking and planning this was the result: Frolic was selected as being the best-behaved of the two mules; the double crate was harnessed to her back, and in each crate a little cub was secured. The pelts of the bear, the panther, and the lynx were strapped across her back, and she was ready to start back to Long's Peak village, with Mr. Lewis and Omney. There the bears would be crated anew, and shipped to the Zoo at Central Park, New York City, while the pelts were to be expressed to Mrs. Vernon's home to await the scouts' return.

Mr. Lewis was then to send Frolic back with Omney, who was to trail with the party and help Tally in various ways, while his master finished his lecture tour in Colorado.

The morning of their departure, the cubs were scrubbed, combed, and fed to repletion by the scouts, then secured in the crates. They were oblivious of the tears shed by the scouts over their soft little bodies, for they were curled up and fast asleep after such a hearty breakfast.

When Mr. Lewis and Omney rode down the trail, the scouts wept forlornly while the little party was in sight, but once a bend in the pathway was turned, Scrub came in for his full share of love and petting again.

"If we could only have kept the cubs with us!" sighed Joan.

"Thank heavens we have Scrub left as a hostage for Frolic," sighed Ruth, hugging the dog, who *now* ignored every fond attention.

"As it was impossible to 'travel light' with two bears, isn't it much better the way we arranged it, girls?" asked Mrs. Vernon.

And they had to admit that such was the case.

CHAPTER NINE
A THRILLING CANOE TRIP

With one pack mule less, Jolt had more to carry but he seemed not to mind it. He was made up of that temperament like few humans, that as long as he had plenty to eat and a place to sleep, it mattered not how hard he had to work at other times.

The day following Mr. Lewis's departure with Omney and the cubs, the scouts broke camp and moved along the trail to pitch a camp nearer Battle Mountain. From this spot Mr. Gilroy and Mr. Vernon could daily rove about, hunting for the precious bits of rock and débris that meant so much to the geologist. Here the party planned to await the return of Omney and the mule, Frolic.

The new camp near Battle Mountain was much like the old one, with the exception of its being nearer the trail instead of way back in the woods. Thus it happened that the second day of camping, a party of tourists stopped to ask which trail would lead them to a certain stream where they were to meet a party of canoeists.

Tally explained how they could reach the place, and after they had gone, Joan sighed, "I wish we could canoe for a change!"

"It wouldn't be much like the infant trips we took last summer," said Ruth.

"I should say not! In the Rockies there'd be rapids, then a whirlpool, and then over a waterfall—to extinction!" laughed Julie.

"All the same, others take these trips safely,—why shouldn't experienced scouts?" added Anne.

"Just because we never thought of it, with all our other excitement," answered Ruth.

"Now that we have thought of it, let's ask Verny why there are no places where one can hire a canoe," suggested Julie.

The girls laughed at such an idea, but the thought of what a wonderful experience it would be to canoe on these streams, clung to their minds, and so the Captain heard about it.

"Even if you had canoes, there are no navigable streams," said she.

"Those folks who stopped to ask Tally the way to Flat Top base were to meet friends who canoed all the way from somewhere," said Joan.

"Yes, they told us they were to meet the party there and all were going to cross the Divide on horses, then come back and canoe home," added Judith.

"It seems too bad that all those fine canoes must remain idle while those folks are riding over the Divide," sighed Julie.

Mrs. Vernon purposely ignored the sigh and the insinuation, then did her best to change the subject to one more practical. But the Fates were against her this time.

The following morning, two of the men who had previously stopped to inquire the right trail to take, returned to ask Tally if he knew of any one who would sell them, or hire out, a number of mountain-climbing horses. Now that the canoeing party had arrived, there were no extra horses for them to ride.

"How many horses will you need?" asked Julie, quickly scheming.

"There are eight people in the party, and they will want one or two extra horses for the luggage," replied the man.

"There are nine horses and one mule in *our* outfit," hinted Julie, her eyes gleaming as she glanced at the Captain.

"But your mounts will do us no good," laughed the man.

"Oh, they might, if you could persuade us to swap for a time," said Julie, daringly.

"Julie, what *do you* mean?" demanded Mrs. Vernon, angrily.

"Why, one likes to be brotherly, you know, Verny, and in the wilds, far from other people, we ought to do a good turn to strangers. Here is a party with a number of canoes but no horses, and here are we with horses but no canoes—see my point?" she said.

"Even though you are the Scout Leader, Julie, I do not see how you can even suggest such a step. The Captain refuses to listen to any argument along those lines," said Mrs. Vernon sternly.

"We scouts like to canoe, and we will be here at camp for several weeks, so a little side trip like the one offered now would be most delightful," responded Julie, who understood that the Captain's objections arose mostly from dread of the scouts taking the trip on unknown streams.

"Several weeks! Why, we are only camping here for a few days," retorted Mrs. Vernon. "Besides I have no idea of exchanging safe methods of travel, for what is known to be a great risk."

"Verny, Gilly told Uncle last night that he had enough material on hand in these moraines to keep him busy for a year, if he wanted to do the thing properly. But even as it was, he proposed spending several weeks between here and Tyndall Glacier," said Joan, to corroborate Julie's statement.

"Well, what of that? Would you advise me to loan the horses Gilly gave security for, to a party of strangers we never saw in our lives?"

Before any one could answer, Mr. Gilroy hurried back to camp. "I've forgotten my magnifying glasses, girls. Don't stop me for anything, now," said he.

He ran into his tent and was out again in a moment, but one of the men who came to ask about horses, recognized him in that moment.

"Why, it is Mr. Gilroy, who has a place in the Adirondacks!" exclaimed he, coming forward.

"Well of all people! You're the last I looked for in the Rockies, Kenmore!" laughed Mr. Gilroy, shaking hands with his friend from the East.

"Funny how we should happen to meet like this," said Mr. Kenmore, then he introduced his companion. Mr. Gilroy, in turn, introduced the two men to Mrs. Vernon and the girls.

When Mr. Kenmore told his story, and why he had stopped at the camp, Julie hastily interpolated and repeated what she had said about a fair exchange of horses and canoes. But no one spoke of the Captain's fears.

"Say, Ken, that plan might work out all right," declared Mr. Gilroy. "How long shall you folks want to use the horses?"

"Why, as to that—we can go as far as your time permits, and return when you say."

"Well, I'll tell you! I've got to be about these diggings for another ten days or two weeks at least, and if the scouts want to take a little canoe trip during that time, I think it will be fine! What do you say, Captain?" and Mr. Gilroy turned to Mrs. Vernon.

"You seem to have settled everything before you asked my opinion. Yet there would be no scouts in the Rockies if I were not responsible for each one of them on this trip!"

"Why, Captain! I imagined you were as eager for this trip as the girls seem to be!" exclaimed Mr. Gilroy, aghast.

"Eager—what for? Losing half the scouts in a whirlpool because of a silly notion of Juliet's?" The very mention of Julie's full name sobered every one considerably, for they realized that the Captain was very serious in her objecting to this new risk.

Mr. Gilroy suggested, "Can you two men spend the day with Mrs. Vernon and the scouts? I've simply *got* to rush away and meet Mr. Vernon. Then we will plan to-night after dinner, and see what we can do. I do know that there's no use your trailing back unless you go all the way to Loveland or Boulder for your mounts—and you won't want to lose all that time, I'm sure."

So Mr. Kenmore and his friend, Mr. Neil, spent a pleasant day with the scouts, and at night the subject of canoeing was again debated.

Finally, Joan said, "It's foolish of Verny to say we will drown, when we won badges for our canoeing last year, and carried off the prizes for our county this spring."

"These girls are better swimmers and more expert canoeists than most," added Mr. Gilroy.

"Besides, my dear," said Mr. Vernon to his wife, "it is not as if they had to paddle. With expert Indians to guide the crafts, why do you feel so timid about the trip?"

"We only have Tally, and he can paddle but one canoe at a time. If only Omney were here, he could take charge of one, and I could manage the other one," sighed Mrs. Vernon, feeling overcome by the combined arguments of the others.

"How many canoes have you?" asked Mr. Gilroy.

"Three large ones, built for parties," replied Mr. Kenmore. "My wife is a poor swimmer and knows nothing about a canoe, yet she had no fear in trusting herself to the expert Indian who managed the canoe she was in."

"Why not let that Indian take charge of one canoe? Then the Captain will feel safer, and her responsibility will be less?" suggested Mr. Gilroy.

"We'd be glad to, as that will take care of him until we come back from our ride."

Finally, Mrs. Vernon said, "If you agree to wait until Omney returns, so we can let him manage one of the canoes, I'll withdraw most of my objections, but still I am not in favor of this trip!"

Having gained that much, the scouts knew better than to urge more at that time. Mr. Kenmore was relieved to find he could go back to his party with such good news—that horses and pack-mules were found as if by a fairy. He thought to himself, "By a clever little scout of a fairy, called Julie!"

Before the two men left camp in the morning, it was all settled. As soon as Omney returned, the scouts would break camp and ride on until they reached the camp pitched by Mr. Kenmore's party. Mr. Gilroy and Mr. Vernon would move leisurely along, searching in the moraines during the day, and pitching camp wherever they were when night fell. There would be no outfits to look after, and no cares about scouts, so they would reach Flat Top about the time the canoe party returned from its trip.

As soon as Omney came back to camp, therefore, every one was ready to proceed along the trail to Kenmore's Camp. When the scout party rode into that camp, every one there was glad to see them, for they had heard about the scout outing and the plan to exchange horses for canoes, for a short time, at least.

"Couldn't be better if Providence itself planned it all!" declared Mrs. Kenmore, enthusiastically. "Don't you think so, Mrs. Vernon?"

"I'll wait until we return before I commit myself. I always did think folks blamed Providence too much for what really was their own stubborn will," returned the Captain.

Her repartee caused a laugh, and Julie exclaimed, "Verny, I fear you are coming down with chills and fever,—you never were so pessimistic before!"

"Yes, you are awfully lugubrious, Verny. At home you are with us on any wildcat scheme," added Ruth.

"That's it! It took a trip to the Rockies to show me what I was at home—for your wildcat schemes. Now I'm learning sense!" declared the Captain.

Mr. Kenmore had a brilliant idea, and he instantly followed it up. He brought the Indian guide who had paddled the canoe to camp, and introduced him to Mrs. Vernon, as his future mistress for the canoe trip.

The Captain saw the tall slender form, the fine muscular development of the Indian, and the polite demeanor. Then she said, "Have you been in the Rockies long?"

"Borned here. My fodder Chief of waterways in Colorado when she was territory and me lee'l boy." The Indian demonstrated how small he was at that time.

"John tells me he has spent the last twenty years on these streams flowing from the Rockies. So he can be depended upon," said Mr. Kenmore.

That noon, the party wishing to cross the Divide rode away with the horses and two pack-mules, while the three Indian guides showed Mrs. Vernon the route they proposed taking for the canoe trip. They would follow the creek that eventually emptied its crystal waters into Glacier Creek. But the latter had many fine tributaries, so they would follow one of these to a spot John knew of, where a short carry of a mile would bring them to a splendid river along which they could canoe for miles and miles.

The blankets and other necessities were carefully packed in the bottom of the canoes, and the slat frameworks for the flooring were laid down over them. Then the scouts divided their party and got into the three large canoes, with an experienced guide for each.

When they were once under way, Mrs. Vernon began to enjoy the trip as much as any one of the scouts. She leaned back comfortably in the canoe as she thought to herself, "What's so enjoyable as this peaceful riding over placid waters, and passing by Nature's wonder-spots!"

The Indians thoroughly enjoyed canoeing, and the two boys, Tally and Omney, were delighted at the change of plan that made this water trip possible for them. The paddles were in capable hands, and the canoes responded instantly to every touch.

A stroke one way and the canoe would evade a snag thrusting its ugly head from the stream. A stroke the other way, and the passengers quickly rounded a finger of land that jutted out into the water. Now and then a quick stroke, and a rock was passed without scraping, and all was done so quietly that no undue fear was roused.

They rode under massive overhanging rocks, glided past flat banks of land where gorgeous bloom offered sweetest nectar to bees and butterflies. Then they would shoot by cliffs whose towering sides were bare and threatening, or were overrun with vines and topped with giant pines whose roots found a hold down on the other side of the rock.

Finally the current began to run swifter, and still swifter. The Captain sat, half-mesmerized by the swirling water as the canoe shot through it. She was in a delicious state of mind when a stifled scream from Julie, in the leading canoe, caused her to rouse instantly.

They were sweeping around a wooded curve in the stream, and just before them was a series of little rapids that foamed and frothed. Farther on a narrow gorge was seen, and here the water doubled on itself and curled backward in its attempt to escape from the frowning walls of rock on either side.

Now the canoes were in the white churning waters! Now they were cutting through the foam, the wavelets striving to pile up and over the top of the canoes. The rapids roared as they flung themselves against the rocky wall just ahead, and the Captain murmured, "Oh, I hope no one runs into that!"

Then the three canoes were flying through the gorge, riding over the lapping waters, and now they were out again on the other side, gliding silently across a wide expanse of dark-green lake. And now the Captain heaved a sigh of relief and sent up a prayer of thanks for the protection.

The lake was quickly crossed, and again the three canoes were going down what seemed to be a chute. The scouts gasped at the speed, and grasped the edges of the crafts tightly. When the first canoe, managed by John, came to the spot, he called back a warning to the other two guides. And all three bent their muscles to the work in hand.

Suddenly, without other warning, Mrs. Vernon felt as if the canoe she sat in had dropped from under her—its flight was so swift that she scarcely realized the motion. Then—s-s-suash! down it came upon the top of the water again—but far ahead of whence it sprang. She turned to look at what could have caused this queer sensation and saw they had ridden a "rift."

The three Indians cheered and complimented the scouts for their courage in this their first rift. So the scouts understood that such things were mere joys to an Indian and nothing to be frightened about.

During the afternoon the line of canoes reached one of the wildest and most alluring spots in the mountains. The forest was not so dense here, the water was smoother, and the stream wider. The Indians were warning each other "Watch out!" so their passengers were alert also. No one wanted to miss a single thrill of this marvelous trip.

Now a sound as of thunder in the distance reached their ears, and the Captain wondered what it could be. As the canoes sped onward, the sound grew plainer and louder, and caused a clutch of fear at the throats of the girls. But the Indians smiled eagerly and allayed undue trepidation.

Then quite suddenly, coming out of a screen of overhanging verdure, the strange sounds broke into wild tearing, roaring, pulsating tones, and the canoes slid down upon the tawny yellow chute of a *real* cataract!

The bulky black things that flashed up before the canoes, only to be as swiftly passed by, were *rocks*! The queer, rocking, green-gold glass they were sliding upon was *water*! And then, as in the rift, after a sudden sinking as if through space, they all rode out safely upon another deep quiet lake of dark-green water.

That night the Indians made camp on the moonlit shores of a marvelous lake. They had not bothered to stop for much dinner at noon, so every one was hungry by evening. Freshly caught fish, and the food that only an Indian can find and cook to perfection, made the scouts feel "like monarchs of all they surveyed."

Such thrilling experiences as John could tell, kept the scouts gasping until Mrs. Vernon suggested they had best go to bed if they wished to continue in the morning. The beds of sweet bracken made up by Tally never held more appreciative mortals than the scouts, after the entertainment furnished by John had ended.

For breakfast, there were wild ducks' eggs, found by Omney; stewed Indian potatoes, dug by Tally; Indian onions, discovered by John; and delicious coffee, brought by Mrs. Vernon. Then they cleared away all signs of the camp and proceeded along the way.

The second day of the canoeing there was no fear felt by any one, as the Indians had proved to be adequate for any emergency, and the canoes were splendidly constructed craft. In them the scouts shot rapids, rode down cataracts, bobbed about in whirlpools, and then—rode out upon quiet lakes laughing merrily in their nervous tension.

Finally Julie felt tired of sitting still, and asked to paddle. But the guides shook their heads. No amount of coaxing could make them turn over the paddles to other hands. The Indians knew their responsibility, and were determined to avoid trouble.

The third morning, Julie said, "We can paddle so well, Tally, and some of these lakes are as tame as dish-water."

"Den wait to dinnertime at camp!" said Tally, unthinkingly.

The rest of the morning was passed in dodging great rocks, passing through arched aisles, where the water cut a way through the timber, or again rocking perilously in a seething bowl of froth, to be shot out at the other side, and then ride along on smooth water.

That noonday they landed on a blossoming meadow for camp. The canoes were taken from the water and turned over on the beach, while the Indians hunted for food to cook for dinner. Two of them started for an inland pond where they saw flocks of wild duck, and John began to catch fish for cooking.

Mrs. Vernon took charge of the fire, and the scouts made bread, set the dishes out and did other chores. Julie and Joan had been sent to hunt for a fresh spring of water, and in passing the canoes where they had been left, Joan said, "The lake's like a millpond."

"I'd like to paddle across to the other side and climb that steep knoll. I bet there's a fine view from there," said Julie.

"Verny would have a fit!" declared Joan, looking back but not seeing the camp, as the bank hid it from sight.

"It wouldn't take long, and I'm dying to try these canoes," suggested Julie.

"Come on, then," responded Joan. "I suppose it's safe."

"Of course, and Tally said we might try at noon-time."

"We'll just shoot over and back again," said Joan, as the two girls managed to carry the canoe to the water.

No one saw them glide away, and no one missed them at first, as they were thought to be hunting for spring water. Then when dinner was ready there was no Julie or Joan to be found!

CHAPTER TEN
JULIE AND JOAN'S PREDICAMENT

It was all very well to talk about paddling across a quiet little lake, but it was another thing when one got into the swift current that ran past the rocky bluff where the girls wished to land. There was no shallow water anywhere, where they might get out and beach the canoe, so Julie paddled with the current for a distance, leaving the camp site far behind.

Joan kept gazing for a likely spot to anchor in, but there were none such. Then suddenly, the canoe was caught in a swirl of water that was caused by the outpouring of a creek, and Julie discovered that managing a large canoe built for Rocky Mountain waters was far different from steering a light craft across a home lake, or along the canal that ran through the town.

"Why are you going this way, Julie—why not stick to the shore line?" asked Joan, as the canoe was driven along with the current.

"Stick to nothing! How can I help going this way when the current is as mad as a Jehu!" cried Julie, desperately.

"Then let me help in some way."

"I only wish you could, but we only have one paddle."

Joan glanced at the water. It was running quite shallow just where they were. An idea flashed into her mind.

"Julie, I'll get out and pull the canoe upstream while you help with the paddle."

Julie made no demur, although she said, warningly, "Don't let go of the canoe for a second, will you?"

"Of course not! Did you think I wanted to be left on a desert shore?" laughed Joan, climbing out.

She managed to drag the canoe for quite a distance upstream again, while Julie paddled with all her might. At times Joan stepped down in a hole and had to cling to the canoe to save herself. At such times the craft swung back again downstream, making the girls do the same work all over again. Finally Joan's teeth began chattering and she managed to quiver forth, "The water's like ice!"

"You've been in too long. Now you get in and let me take your place, Jo. Later you can switch off with me again, and in that way we'll get back to still water opposite camp."

So Julie jumped out and Joan got in to paddle, but her hands were stiff with the chill and her whole body shaking, hence her paddling was not of much use. Julie was the stronger of the two scouts, so she managed to pull the canoe upstream splendidly, and both girls felt that now their troubles were over. All of a sudden, however, she stumbled over a great submerged stone and fell out flat on the water, face downward.

She had presence of mind to cling to the edge of the canoe with both hands, but Joan stopped paddling in consternation when she saw the accident. Instantly the craft caught in the swift current and shot ahead as an arrow from the bow. Julie floated out behind, on the water, at times completely covered with the swirling waves curled up by the sharp canoe.

At times she lifted her head up and tried to gasp. In one of these desperate efforts, she cried, "Paddle—paddle for the love of Mike!" then she was swept under again.

Before Joan got down to actual work again with the paddle, the canoe was running opposite the creek again, and all the gain the girls had made by wading upstream was lost. Julie was very cold by this time, and the water was so deep that she could not touch bottom, so she climbed back in the canoe.

During the help Joan had to give the half-fainting mariner, the canoe headed straight for a bend in the river. Where they would land neither scout could tell. It might be over the falls—it might be in a mud puddle.

"Can't you stop it?" screamed Julie, hysterically. "We may run plumb into a cliff and smash to bits!"

As she spoke, she grabbed the paddle and worked with the strength that fear sometimes gives, so that she really poled the canoe across the creek to the shore where the water was quiet. But they were now on the far side of the current, in the creek that was hidden by the bluff they had passed. The distance from camp was too far for any one to hear them, even if they did shout. So they fastened the canoe and got out upon the bank.

"When Verny finds us gone, and one canoe missing, she will send the Indians out at once to hunt for us. Meantime, we may as well make a fire and get warm," suggested Julie.

"Tally left a line and tackle in the bottom of the canoe," announced Joan, remembering that she had caught her toe on a fish-hook when she climbed out.

"Oh, then we're not so hard up, after all. We can catch a fish and broil it for lunch."

"I'm fearfully hungry after all that work," hinted Joan.

"Then you fish while I make fire with some rubbing-sticks. As soon as you land a fish, I'll clean it with my scout knife and start broiling it. Better try upstream a ways, where the water is quiet," said Julie.

The fire was soon blazing, and Joan managed to catch two goodly sized fish, so they ate them, and dried their uniforms at the fire at the same time. This done, they felt better. But no call from the rescuers the girls had expected, nor sign of them, came from the lake beyond the bluff.

"Jo, suppose we follow this creek a ways until we find a shallow place where we can ford. Then we can climb up to that knoll and signal with smokes."

"We may get into all sorts of new trouble, Julie. I'd rather wait here for them."

"I've got to get up and do something, Jo. I'll go crazy sitting here waiting, with no sign from any one out there."

"Why can't we paddle the canoe up a ways. If we walk we may step on a rattler, or meet other dreadful things," ventured Jo.

"All right, then. We'll canoe upstream a ways. If it doesn't look healthy yonder, we'll come back. But should we find a trail we may as well follow it to the bluff," returned Julie.

"Who'd make a trail in this wilderness!" scorned Joan.

"Don't you suppose others have been in this beautiful spot? Others have seen that bluff and climbed it, too."

So the scouts paddled the canoe upstream as far as it seemed advisable, and that is how they missed hearing the Indians, when they crossed the creek and called for the lost ones. Then the hunters paddled on downstream, searching ahead for a canoe that might be going straight for the great falls John knew to be a mile further down.

John and Omney were in the leading canoe, while the Captain and Tally were in the second canoe of the rescuing party. When no sign of the scouts was seen at the creek, John called back to Tally.

"Omney and me go on, you take lady to shore and wait on creek for me."

Tally did not tell Mrs. Vernon that a dangerous waterfall was downstream, but he knew that was where John was going to hunt, so he landed his passenger on the far side of the creek, where they sat and waited for news. No one dreamed that the two girls would paddle up the creek and thus miss a chance of being helped. Nor did Tally find the ashes of the little campfire Julie had made to cook the fish and to dry themselves.

"I knew there would be a fine trail along here, somewhere, Jo!" exclaimed Julie, driving the canoe inshore and pointing exultantly at a distinct trail that ran up from the water's edge.

"Oh, joy! It runs straight for the bluff, too!" cried Joan.

So they climbed this steep trail, which was so plainly worn that there was no need of blazes along the way. They climbed and climbed! Still they had not reached the top where they expected to find the knoll they originally started out for.

"Seems to me we have gone twice as far as ever that bluff was," complained Joan.

"Places always seem close at hand when one is on the water," commented Julie.

But they now found the trail descending, and shortly it went decidedly downhill, away from the lake. Both scouts looked at each other.

"There is no sense in *going down*, Julie!"

"Apparently not, Jo, but these trails wind awfully, you know; and maybe it is trying to avoid a gully or a cliff."

So they kept on, hoping every moment for a sight of the bald place that had allured them from the camp on the safe and desirable meadow. After half an hour of this hiking they came out to an inland pond with canals cut in different directions.

"Why! it's a beaver colony!" exclaimed Julie, pointing to the huts and dam, and they saw several beavers working in the aspens at the far side of the pond.

"I could eat one of those beavers—I'm so starved!" sighed Joan.

"Shall we follow that trail around the pond?" asked Julie.

"What for? We're only going further away all the time."

"Then we may as well go back to the creek and wait."

"All this long walk for nothing!" grumbled Joan. But she followed Julie nevertheless, and when they reached the brook they had recently crossed, the girls found two trails leading to it.

"I only saw one before," said Joan.

"Because we were *on* that one,—but which one was it?"

"Coming from the left, to be sure. Would we be coming from the interior?" asked Joan, impatiently.

So they took the lefthand trail, although they really had come up by the other one, which led from the creek where their canoe was waiting.

"Jo, I believe both those trails were worn by animals going to the creek," ventured Julie, as the idea suddenly came to her.

"Well, you said tourists would surely visit here and leave a trail!" Joan returned, jeeringly.

For once Julie made no reply in self-justification. The two scouts kept on hiking until they were so fatigued that they both felt like crying.

"I hope we're not lost," whimpered Joan, wiping her eyes.

"Of course not! Folks are never lost unless they get into a panic of fear," declared Julie, keeping up her own courage by trying to boost that of her companion.

Again the girls climbed and climbed, until presto! right in front and down far below, was the lovely lake! Oh, how beautiful it looked! They stood where they were for a few moments sighing in relief that now they were sure to be rescued. Then Julie frowned and looked at Joan.

"Jo, is there anything wrong with my eyes? I can't see any meadow opposite us."

"Neither can I! There's a rocky pine-topped wall over there."

"But there *was* a flat meadow where we camped, wasn't there?" queried Julie.

"O Julie, you're not going daffy, are you?" wailed Joan.

"Good gracious! Why do you ask such a thing! *Was* there a meadow over there?" screamed Julie, shaking Joan fearfully.

"I've heard that folks lose their minds when they're lost in the wilderness," cried Joan, forgetting to answer the all-important question about the meadow.

"Will you tell me what I want to know—*was there a meadow*?" yelled Julie, stamping her foot vehemently as she spoke.

She had been standing upon long wiry witch grass that had washed its blades downwards toward the lake, and having but little roothold in the thin layer of dried moss and top soil that was spread over the cliff, the sharp stamping of a scout heel loosened this slight attachment.

Then like a mirage in the desert, Joan beheld her friend vanish! Not swiftly and instantaneously, but slowly and surely, as the roots and matted surface reluctantly broke away because of Julie's weight and downward gravity.

"Save me! Oh Jo! Save me!" screamed Julie, clutching wildly at scrub bushes that held tenaciously to the crevices and so gave her temporary resistance. But her weight always tore them away finally, and then she had to grasp the next one.

"Oh Julie—come back! Come back, don't leave me all alone in this wilderness!" wailed Joan, wringing her hands.

The sudden realization that Joan thought only of herself in face of the calamity that threatened her friend, served to cool Julie's fear; then she used common sense in sparing herself as far as possible. She was out of Joan's sight now, and by making use of every bush, root, or vine on the slanting rocks, she resisted the force of gravitation enough to slide slowly instead of being catapulted from the heights. She knew not just where this chute would end—in deep or shallow water. If the former she still might swim to shore, if that were not too far away.

The last few feet of this slide ended abruptly where the cliff had been worn away by the spring freshets and floods. Here Julie dropped into the water which formed a hole along the rockbound shore, so that she went in without striking anything, and immediately began swimming to free herself from the tangle of roots and débris that fell with her.

She swam for a distance until she found a narrow edge of sand where she might sit and rest in the sunshine. So she managed to reach this twenty-inch-wide refuge and shook out her hair to dry. She wondered what Joan would do when she found she had to make her own way alone to the canoe! And the picture she painted of her erstwhile companion, stumbling along weeping, gave her some satisfaction.

This spirit of vengeance, however, was soon gone, and a kindly feeling took its place. She began to plan how she might creep along that narrow edge of beach to reach the point on land where she could see the creek pouring into the lake. From there she could signal Joan when she reached the canoe, and thus relieve her mind of the fear that her chum had been drowned.

After overcoming many obstacles, she reached the jutting land that marked the entrance to the creek. The canoe had landed on the opposite side, further up stream. Hardly had she gained the top of this promontory before she heard excited voices, and one above the others wailing dismally.

Instantly she knew Joan was safe and that the others had arrived. A line of Scripture flashed through her mind and caused her to smile—"The voice of one crying in the wilderness," quoth Julie.

No sooner had she grasped the fact that she would be with her old friends in a few moments, than she recovered all her old *sang froid*. She shook out her clinging clothes, and twisted up her half-dried hair, then sat down on top of the promontory and sang. Yes, *sang*, and sang merrily, too, because she thought that would convey the impression of how unconcerned she felt.

Sound carries far over the water, so Julie's singing was heard by the rescuers as soon as they came out into the lake. Then they shouted, and she replied. Finally they saw the solitary figure sitting upon a rock with both hands clasped about her knees, singing as if her heart was too full of joy to hold it all.

The moment the canoes came near enough, the Captain gazed up, and asked, "How can you get down, Julie?"

"Same way I came up, Verny—with my feet!"

Every one laughed, but Mrs. Vernon shook her head as she murmured, "Same old Julie! Nothing on earth will quench that spirit."

Suddenly, to the horror of every one in the canoes, they saw a form shoot past them and dive into the water. But as suddenly, a laughing face appeared above the surface and soon Julie was in one of the canoes.

Had it not been for the danger of upsetting, the occupants of that canoe would have hugged the scout in their relief at having found her safe and sound,—because Joan's report had been more than despairing.

"O Julie, darling! I thought you were dead!" cried Joan.

"Did you? But you wailed for yourself when you saw me go down to perdition," scorned Julie.

"But how did you manage to get down to the promontory, Julie?" argued Joan, ignoring the other's reply.

"Now, how do you s'pose? I motored there, of course!"

When they all returned to the belated and cold dinner, it was late afternoon, and no one felt in the mood for fresh adventures that day. So they decided to camp on the lovely meadow for the night, and continue the trip in the morning. The three scouts who had been left in camp to guard the dinner were not told of the escape until later.

As they all dawdled languidly over the last fragments of the supper, a silver bar slanted suddenly across their faces, and the very dishes were transformed into a shimmering glory. The broad shaft of light that shone from the newly-risen moon lighted up the whole meadow and penetrated far into the dark fringe of pines that bordered the meadowland.

Then the full moon rose higher in the vaulted dome of the blue heavens—heavens as blue as the Venetian Sea; and sharp points of starlight began to twinkle like tiny beacons on crafts at anchor in that peaceful haven of fathomless blue.

CHAPTER ELEVEN
ON TO FLAT TOP MOUNTAIN

What would a trip in the Rockies mean without an Indian guide? He is the most valuable asset one can have. No matter where he finds himself, under the greatest stress of difficult conditions and circumstances, the Indian guide will manage to save the day. No human being can get as much out of Nature as an Indian. No one can find as desirable a campsite without loss of time. No one can make fire as quickly, pitch tents so securely, weave beds so comfortably, clean up so neatly, spin yarns so thrillingly, and smoke a pipe so contentedly, as an Indian.

So, in the early morning when the scouts awakened to the hope of new adventures, they found their guides preparing breakfast. Julie and Joan felt no after-effects of their unpleasant experience, other than in memory, and there was no reason for that to cripple either one.

The breadtwists were baking, duck broiling, and other delicious odors coming from the campfire, so the girls speedily completed their bath and toilet for the day. Then, the delicious breakfast out of the way, the kits were packed into the canoes, the scouts got in and sat down, and onward they traveled.

At every turn in the stream new vistas of Nature's varied beauties opened out before their admiring eyes, and every now and then, a scout would call, "Take that picture, Verny! It's wonderful." And the Captain always snapped the scene.

Beautiful birds swung low on branches, with heads on one side, eyeing the strange creatures in the canoes. Squirrels sat upon the boughs and threw nutshells at the scouts as the canoes passed under their perches. Thus the hours flew by until night fell again. Camp was made, supper cooked, Indian legends told about the fire, then bed and refreshing sleep.

Beautiful weather blessed the scouts while on the canoe trip, and added to the enjoyment of the experience. Many times they paddled through water that looked like molten silver, so heavy and opaque was it in the weird light. Again they went along streams that reflected the sunset hues, and looked more like sheets of opal with its changeable colors of rose, lilac, and yellow-green. Then this fading, translucent color would suddenly vanish, and all be dark! Again there were times when the canoes threaded a way between towering cliffs that cast somber shadows down upon the waters, and other times when they rushed through gorges and gullies.

Hour after hour, day after day, sped on to join the yesterdays, with one thrilling experience after another passing into memories, and the scouts began to realize that their trip was almost ended. All the time the three Indians paddled faithfully, carefully, and silently, as much a factor in the enjoyment of the marvelous scenes as the water or the forests.

At last the scouts reached the great falls that marked the end of the journey, but they still had the joy of going back. So the backtrail began, with as many happy adventures as one can hope for on a canoe trip. No accident or disagreement marred the trip, and when they reached the rendezvous where they were to meet the riders who went over the Divide, every one was satisfied.

"'The End of a Perfect Day,'" sang Julie, as she jumped out of the canoe.

That same night Mr. Gilroy and Mr. Vernon hiked into camp and were received with noisy welcome. They were as wildly enthusiastic over the fine specimens they had secured in their side trips, as the scouts were over their canoe trip. Then in the morning the riders came to camp, and after hearty thanks from both sides, the horses and canoes changed hands again.

The Kenmore party started down the stream, and the scouts rode away along the trail that led to Glacier Creek and to Flat Top Mountain. The trails were rough but the horses were sure-footed, and all went well.

They had gone some distance when just ahead, beside the trail they were following, they saw a beautiful sheet of water. It really was a wild tarn, placed in the pocket of the mountains that encircled it.

"It looks just like a diamond sparkling in the deep prongs of these pointed peaks," said Julie.

"We've discovered a poetess, scouts!" exclaimed Ruth, but Julie frowned upon her.

"We'll find many such pure jewels hidden in these settings," said Mr. Gilroy. "Some are perched so high in the mountaintops that you wonder how they ever snuggle there. Others are so deeply entrenched in terrifying chasms and ravines that only the intrepid ever see them. But most of these gems are made by the glaciers that carved out their basins by constant friction. The waters, so cold and pure, come from leaping cataracts and icy falls above, that flow from the melting ice fields during the summer."

On the shores of one of these lovely lakes the Indians made camp that night. The two scientists decided to study some of the peculiar formations found near the place, and the scouts were satisfied to enjoy a quiet rest for a time. With an acre or more of flower-dotted meadow on one side, rugged cliffs on another side, dark forests on still the third side, and Tyndall Glacier rising sheer from the fourth side, what more could adventurous youth ask?

"Girls," remarked Mr. Gilroy that evening, "this place offers us all we need for individual pastimes,—you to explore in the forests, and Vernon and I to collect specimens. It's up to you to say how long we camp here. I'm ready to move on whenever you say."

Later, as they sat about the campfire, Betty asked, "Gilly, what is it that makes a glacier?"

"Is it the winter's snow that piles up on mountaintops and freezes?" added Julie who, too, had been puzzling over the matter.

"A glacier, girls, is an accumulation of ice in an altitude where the melting process is not equal to the deposit. Every winter adds snow and ice to the peaks, and then when these slide down to milder areas, they melt and vanish into these rivers and tarns.

"Some of these glaciers found in the Rockies were left here since the Ice Age, when the whole globe was ice-clad. The glacial rivers that flowed from these ice-peaks are mainly responsible for the wild scenery in these mountains. They cut a gully here, or scoop out a pit there, according to the force and size of the torrents. In thus forcing a way through every obstacle, these resistless currents carry along timber, soil, and rocks.

"These, in turn, tearing and banging against other obstacles that resist them, finally carry *them* along to add to the power of its ruthless progress.

"Through ages these ice torrents, starting from the highest peaks and coming down, down, down from one resting place to another, but always traveling downward and onward, moving mountains, as it were, changing the course of mighty rivers, filling up inland seas,—have given you this grand scenery of to-day.

"Not only do all kinds of débris come flooding the valleys and lakes with this gushing from glacial fields, but gold and other precious metals are washed down and deposited. Thus the seeker may find gold, if he is willing to sacrifice for it.

"To warn you scouts that these glacial fields are not as safe as a floor in your home, let me tell you what happened to a party of mountain climbers. They were experienced men, too.

"They were climbing Mont Blanc when a snowslide swept them away into a deep crevasse. One man escaped to tell the story. It was impossible to reach any of them, so the scientists figured out how long a time must elapse before the glacier would move down to give up its victims. Computations had it that forty years must pass by and then the ice would reach a place where the bodies of the men would be recovered. Forty-one years afterwards, far down the slope of that same mountain, the frozen forms of seven men were found and removed."

"Well, Gilly, rest assured that not one scout will be found frozen that way, this year or forty years hence!" promised Julie, emphatically.

"Not if we can help it!" seconded the girls.

"See that you remember this vow, when you feel like a little adventuring over a peak," laughed Mr. Gilroy.

A few days after this talk, the scouts begged the guides to take them on a hunting-trip,—not that they ever shot anything, but they liked to explore the forests and watch the animals browse or run away.

So they hiked up the steep ascent of the mountain that rose many thousands of feet above the camp, and after startling several hares and other tiny creatures, they came upon a fox, dining upon a wild rabbit. But he leaped away almost before they had seen him, his great red brush disappearing between the trees.

"Wasn't he splendid!" exclaimed Betty.

"Um! Not scout scare him away—something comin' dis way," returned Tally, peering eagerly into the dimness.

"Tally!" hissed Omney suddenly, "Grizzly!" At the same time the scouts distinctly heard a crashing through the dry branches of the down-timber.

"Clim tree—quick—in any one near!" warned Tally, while he cocked his rifle to protect the scouts.

"Why don't *you*?" demanded Julie, who stood back of the Indians when the other girls scampered anxiously for aspens, or other "safety-first" places.

"Me fight!"

"Oh!" was all Julie said, but she stood her ground behind the two Indians, while her friends all begged her to seek a tree for safety.

"I want to watch what is going on down here—you can't see a thing up in the foliage," called Julie. "Besides, I am safe because the bear will have to down the guides first, before he can get a mouthful out of me."

But the grizzly must have caught a scent of the human beings who stood too near the tempting bit of rabbit right on the trail! So he sat upright on his haunches and waved his fearful paws threateningly, while he growled as if saying, "Come on! I'm waiting for you folks. Why don't you fight?"

But the two guides and Julie were so screened by the bush that the bear could not see them,—he merely scented them. Then the wind shifted again, and the grizzly thought he was mistaken, for he smelled no further annoyance. But he decided to be cautious, as it always behooved him to be when man was at hand. So he gave voice to a terrifying roar, just to show these pigmies what would happen if they dared to interfere with his meal!

Julie stood her ground behind the two Indians

As he sat munching the mouthful of rabbit, blinking at nothing in particular, Tally suddenly jerked his head sideways and took a searching look at the beast. Then he leaned over and whispered to Omney so softly that Julie could not hear a sound.

Omney now stared at the bear in unbelief, but after gazing keenly, soon nodded his head anxiously. Then, in another moment, two rifles were silently levelled, and two shots rang out. The grizzly rolled over while the rabbit still remained half-chewed in his great maw.

"O Tally! Shame on you!" cried Julie, furiously.

The scouts now slid down the treetrunks and ran over. Each one had a protest to register against the heartlessness of the Indians. But they were over by the bear, turning him over on his side.

"Him be Devil-Bear!" exclaimed Tally, excitedly.

"Um! Bump on haid, scar on rump!" added Omney.

"What do you mean, boys?" now asked Mrs. Vernon.

The scouts saw a great knob on one side of the bear's head, and an old scar that cleft his left hind-quarter almost in two.

"Dis ole Devil-Bear come down all time to ranches, kill calf, eat lamb, carry off ennything, an' nobuddy ketch him. Evehbud' hunt and shoot, but Devil-Bear quick an' get away. He climb glacier, go over peaks, live evehwhere.

"Sometime him in Flat Top, nudder time him down in Wyom. One time he run in Denver, kill horse, scare evehbuddy away, den run back to Flat Top." Tally laughed at the last memory.

"Him steal cattle, even fight ranchers, so big reward out fer him," added Omney.

"How can you be sure you have killed this demon?" asked Mrs. Vernon, eagerly.

"We hear 'bout Devil-Bear and pickshers nail on all signboard for reward. Big scar in rump, big lump on haid—him got 'em," Tally replied.

"Um! Dis scar make by rancher. One day he chop wood and fine sheep-dog play round. Devil-Bear steal out of woods, catch dog unner man's nose, and run away. Rancher so mad he frow axe at bear, an' it hit right there," explained Omney, poking his foot at the scar on the bear.

"Rancher say dat bear neveh walk gin, but nex' year nudder rancher see bear kill calf an' many lamb and run away," added Tally.

"Then I'm glad you shot him!" declared Betty, glaring at the dead beast.

"But you've got to get him back to camp, boys, to get the reward," said Mrs. Vernon.

The two Indians considered this the least of their problems, and when they had tied the forelegs and the hindlegs together, they swung the heavy animal from a long pole they had cut down from a clump of pine.

That night when Mr. Gilroy heard the story, he assured the scouts that the guides had really done a great service to the country at large, as this bear had terrorized every one in the mountain ranches.

"As a rule, grizzlies are not ferocious except when interfered with. They use their fine intelligence to keep man at a safe distance with their roaring and display of fierce strength. But this rascal was the exception, and it's well he is dead," added he.

"If the guides get the reward, the scouts ought to have the pelt," suggested Mr. Vernon.

"I'll see to it that they do," returned Mr. Gilroy.

The Indians made quick work of skinning the beast and leaving the head on the body so the bump could be identified. The bear fat was tried out and saved by the guides, and several fine steaks were carved from the carcass and broiled, but the girls refused them.

The men had no such qualms, however, and ate greedily, then smacked their lips laughingly at the disgust manifested on the scouts' faces.

"Devil-Bear good eat!" chuckled Tally, as he wrapped the remaining steaks in a paper for another time.

When the campers resumed their ride, Devil-Bear—or all that was left of him—was packed on Jolt's back. The mule cared not a fig for a dead bear, so the skin was carried along without demur, although the horses now and then caught a whiff of the bear-pelt and tossed their heads nervously.

The trail up Flat Top Mountain proved as wonderful as it had promised to be. The scouts rode their horses without a tremor, although at times they went on narrow ledges, forded roaring streams, or plunged down through gulches, and over down-timber. They steadily climbed all that day, and towards night were on Flat Top—twelve thousand, three hundred feet high.

Mr. Gilroy reached his desired Tyndall Glacier, and so delighted was he that he acted like a boy with a new toy. Here they camped for a few days while the scientist collected some interesting bits, then the party continued to the very top of the mountain.

From this summit the scouts could see over the entire country for miles around. Estes Park looked like a tiny city park from that height. And Long's Peak appeared on a line with their sight. They could plainly see Stone's and Taylor's Peaks, and also Mt. Hallett, while several famous lakes,—Mills, Bierstadt, Dream, and others—were seen gleaming like sheets of blue ice down in the hollows between the crags.

Fresh camp was pitched that night under the shadow of a gigantic column of jagged rock that rose perpendicularly above the tableland of the peak. The base of the rock was about a quarter of a mile around, but one side of the monolith dropped sheer down to a cliff a thousand feet below. From that ledge it again dropped down to another rocky resting-spot hundreds of feet lower. Thence it went straight down three thousand feet to the bottom of its stand, where it found a firm footing in the valley.

As every one was tired with the climb of the day, they were soon fast asleep on the fragrant balsam beds, and slept until the snorting of the horses roused the Indians, and then they, in turn, called to the others to get up.

CHAPTER TWELVE
LOST IN A BLIZZARD

It was early dawn but such dark clouds obscured everything that the scouts thought it still was night.

"Bad storm blowin', Mees'r Gilloy. Us hurry down f'om here," said Tally, anxiously.

"All right—all up, and hurry away!" shouted Mr. Gilroy, running for the horses, to help Omney saddle them for the ride.

Soon thereafter, without stopping to attend to any of their customary toilets, the scouts were in the saddles and quickly following the guides down the trail on the opposite side from that they had mounted the day before.

The blackness was now so thick that it was difficult to see any one ten feet ahead, and the girls could not see the trail at all. Then Tally suddenly shouted a warning to those behind him.

"Huddle togedder—blizzer comin' down now!"

And in a few seconds, an unexpected breaking of the clouds drove thick smothery, enveloping snow across the plateau. Even the heavy clouds seemed to choke everything in their folds. The wind, which blew a gale, uprooted trees and flicked them out of the way as if they were snips of paper. Gusts of the mad tornado tore off great masses of the dark clouds and, eddying them about, whirled the vapor out of them, away down the sides of the mountain. Trees, rocks, clods of earth, everything movable that presented an obstacle to the gale, was carried away like thistledown.

The poor horses and pack-mules crouched close together, with heads low, making of their bodies as scant a resistance as possible against the storm, and at the same time providing shelter, with their steaming bodies, for the human beings who huddled under them.

Then, as suddenly as the storm broke, it ceased. A weird light played over the plateau for a time, and Mr. Gilroy noted the worried expressions of the Indians.

"What now, Tally?"

"Us clim' saddles, stick gedder an' must get away!" shouted Tally, trying to be heard above the soughing of the wind, that was now blowing from behind the crag.

Even as the riders tried to get into the saddles and start after Tally, a chill filled the air. It crept into bones and marrow, and in a few minutes the full fury of the blizzard was felt. In less than five minutes after the first snow fell, everything was drifted under white blankets. The cold bit into human flesh like sharp points of steel, and it was certain that every one must get down from that altitude immediately or be frozen to death.

The Indians led the way, although they trusted their safety on these mountains entirely to the horses and their wonderful sense. The other riders tried to follow as closely as they could in the tracks made by the first two horses. Then as they descended further from the plateau, the storm abated and the temperature felt warmer, until they reached the place where dripping snow from all the tree branches and rocks thoroughly soaked the unfortunates.

The mountainside was cut up by ravines and gulches, or "draws" as they are called, made by erosion of mountain streams that came from the glacier on top of Flat Top.

From one of these draws the scouts could look down for miles to a place where it widened out through the velocity of the roaring waters and unearthed everything in its floods.

Here and there great pines had fallen across and formed natural bridges over the chasms. At other spots the roots or branches of a tree washed down, would catch in the débris of the sides of a draw, obstructing the way and holding up great masses of waste that accumulated rapidly about the twisted limbs, when the torrent washed everything against this comb, that caught the larger objects.

So the file of riders went carefully downward, on the watch for a favorable trail that might lead them to the valley. But every draw they found was so forbidding that they were repulsed from trying it. Some showed great rocks that might roll down at the slightest motion of the ground, and crush everything in their plunge. Even as they pondered the chance of going down one of these, the water caused by the melting snow loosened the grip of a great fragment of rock held up in the gorge, and down it crashed! Other draws displayed century-old snags, and down-timber that lay half-sunken in slimy ooze which trickled down from the mossy sides of the gully; these would suck in any horse or rider that was daring enough to try and go over them.

Finally, Tally came to a draw which was not nearly so forbidding as the others, but it was a very deep chasm, and sent up echoes of roaring water in its bottom.

"Wad yuh tink, Omney—do we try him?" asked Tally.

"Tally, it looks terrifying!" gasped Mrs. Vernon.

"Not so bad as udder ones," remarked Tally.

"Must we go down any of them?" asked Mr. Vernon.

"Mebbe we not find trail for two—four day, and grub mos' gone," returned Tally, meaningly.

"We've got to trust to Tally's guidance, pards, so let us do exactly as he thinks best," added Mr. Gilroy.

Feeling somewhat dubious about the outcome of this ride, the two Indians led down the steep sides of the gulch. The horses slipped, stumbled, and scrambled through the piled-up rubbish until it was a marvel that they had not broken legs and necks. The débris carried down by the streams that emptied into the torrents at the bottom of the draw, formed almost impassable barriers to going onward. But the day was breaking, and this cheered every one tremendously. Soon the darkness would be entirely dispelled and they could see just where the horses were stepping.

"I'm so hungry I could almost eat this leather harness," remarked Anne, sighing.

"Maybe we might catch something for an early breakfast, if we knew where to give our horses a stand while we hunted," said Ruth.

Then, suddenly, they heard a crash of branches and rolling rocks, and there, outlined against the pale sky, stood a giant elk with head erect and ears attentive to the sounds from these riders. It was the first one the scouts had seen, and it was such a magnificent animal that a sight of it was thrilling.

The elk waited with great antlers reared to their extreme height, long sensitive nose sniffing the air, and legs stiffened ready for a leap. The Captain drew the camera from a side-pocket of the saddle and planned to get a picture. But the wary animal heard the click of the shutter and sprang fully fifteen feet across the chasm to gain a ledge of rock that hung dangerously out.

Every one gasped as he waited to see it miss footing, or roll down with the crag that surely would topple over with such added weight upon it. But the elk must have known its trail, for it lightly touched upon the rock, then vanished over the rim of the top.

"There goes our venison steaks for breakfast!" sighed Julie, making the others laugh in spite of their troubles.

The sides of the canyon near the bottom were filled with dangerous sink-holes, or bogs, that were a constant menace to the riders. For let a horse slip into one of these and he might be sucked down instantly. But the animals were sure-footed and accustomed to such rough traveling, and they instinctively avoided all soft soil. Ever and anon, a horse would slip on a rolling stone, or a hoof would break through rotten timber, so that the scouts were being constantly jolted one side or another.

Finally they found better going along a narrow ledge that looked like an old trail. But it began nowhere and ended—well, it terminated suddenly just ahead of Tally's next step!

"Back! Back!" yelled Tally, dragging on the reins with all his might.

That effectually halted the others, who were so close behind him, and Mr. Vernon leaned over to ask, "What is it, Tally?"

"Big hole—she go down mebbe fifty feet to bottom. Gotta back out and go round nudder way."

"Oh, mercy sakes! Back out all along this narrow ledge?" cried the scouts.

But while they spoke, Jolt passed them, going on the verge of the ledge, and causing every one to tremble for his life. When he was passing Tally, the guide shouted angrily, "Whoa! Whoa!"

But Jolt acted exactly like a sleep-walker does. He paid no attention to sight or sound, and in another moment he would have walked right over the edge of the precipice, had not Tally jumped from his saddle and caught hold of the guide rope that had been tied to his halter before entering the gully.

This slight hold, however, did not save the mule from disappearing over the verge of the cliff, and it almost yanked Tally over, too. The only thing that saved the guide was Omney, who jumped to assist his friend when Jolt went by. The rope was instantly wound about a tree stump and braced. Then Tally climbed warily to safety, before the loose shale should crumble in with his weight.

Every one had been speechless with horror a moment before, but now every one spoke with loosened tongue.

"The mule had all the food-stuffs," said Anne.

"And the camp outfit as well," added Mr. Vernon.

"Just think of the poor thing—down there crushed to bits," wept Betty.

Some felt sorry for Jolt, and some felt sorry for themselves. Then Tally said, "Eef light scout crawl ober an' tell what her see Jolt doin', mebbe we save him."

Betty was the lightest so she offered her services. She was tied securely to one of the ropes that hung on the saddle-horn, and Tally advised her what to do.

"Crawl to edge, look down. Tell what Jolt do, or eef he mashed in bottom!"

So Betty crept slowly over the shale and reached the edge of the ravine. She peered down, and the sunlight that shone through the trees just then, helped her to see plainly.

"Jolt's standing on a wide ledge of rock about twenty feet lower than this one. His packs are gone—guess they tumbled down when the straps burst open. But there isn't any *spare* room for him to exercise on," reported Betty.

"Did you say he was standing upon his feet?" asked Mr. Gilroy, unbelievingly.

"Yes, with his head facing towards the outlet of this chasm. He hears me talking, 'cause I see him prick up his long ears."

"Al' light," said Tally, joyfully. "Tell me, do ledge end in hole like dis-a-one do?"

"No, it looks as if it ran right down to the valley, Tally. I can see the sunlight down at the end, about a mile away."

That caused great joy in each heart, and Tally said, "Al'light, now come back."

So the scout crawled back, while Tally spoke with Omney and planned what to do. The result of this conversation was then apparent.

Tally tied a long rope to his own waist, and Omney began paying out the rope as the Indian went over the edge of the gulch. Every one held his breath to wait developments. Then they heard Tally shout, "Al'light—le' go."

"Now us back out—Tally ride Jolt down valley," announced Omney.

"O Hominy! Do you think the mule is all right?" cried Ruth.

"Tally say so. Us go back now." So back they went in every sense of the word—back along the ledge, and backwards all the way.

The horses climbed the rocky slope and went along the top-side of the chasm, but it was no better adapted for comfortable riding than the bottom had been. After an hour of dreadful jumps and jolts and slips, the riders came out to the valley that Betty had spoken of, at the end of the draw.

There stood Tally, grinning with good news. "Fine camp!"

"But where is Jolt?" demanded the scouts.

"Him dockered up wid bear-grease, bandages, an' herb!' laughed Tally, pointing to a place where they could see a mule taking things easy on the grass.

"Got packs out, Tally?" asked Omney.

"Us go in get 'em now, Omney. Scouts make camp an' we come back wid grub, pooty soon."

So the two guides rode in through the chasm again, along the bottom beside the river, and the scouts rode on to make camp where Tally had directed them.

There the scouts found one of the most interesting shelters of all on that camping-trip. It was discovered under the wide overspreading boughs of a clump of firs which had so grown that a perfectly clear and covered area in the center provided a Nature-made house.

While Ruth and Betty were ordered to clean up the sticks and stones on the ground under the trees, the other girls gathered balsam and made the beds. The two men went to fish, and the Captain built a good fire to cook the combination breakfast and dinner, as it was now long past noon.

Tally and Omney came back after a long absence, but they had the packs, a little the worse for the fall, to be sure.

"I see this is the last can of soup and our last can of beans," ventured Mrs. Vernon, when she opened the food-pack.

"Um! Us know rancher—plenty grub in him lodge," said Tally, significantly. Everybody laughed at his wink that accompanied the words.

The ride from Flat Top had been so strenuous that the scouts camped that night in the fir-tree lodge, as they had called it. All retired early, as they hoped to make a start at dawn in order to reach the rancher's, where Tally said he could buy a stock of food.

But a number of timber wolves howled about the camp all the night through, keeping the tired travelers half-awake. Towards dawn they must have followed another scent, as all was quiet in the forests thereafter.

The Captain was startled out of a sound sleep by a strange "s-swish"—close to her ear. Springing up with the remembrance of the wolves, she heard Tally whisper through the pine-boughs, "Tell scout come see caribou in valley."

In a few moments every one was up and out of the tree-lodge. The scouts saw the men crouching down behind a large boulder that stood near the verge of a steep descent to the green valley below. The curious girls soon joined them and then witnessed a most unusual sight.

Down in the valley, several hundred yards away, was a herd of caribou grazing on the juicy grass. A fine buck with antlers spreading far from each side of his head, jumped about as if worked by springs. If a cow got in his way he stamped his polished hoofs and threatened her with his flattened horns.

But the cows seemed not to mind such idle threats on the part of the bull, and continued grazing.

Julie laughed. "They're suffrage caribou—they know how a male talks fine but seldom does what he brags about!"

This started an animated argument between Mr. Gilroy and the Scout Leader, which was suddenly hushed by the behavior of the buck. He lifted his nose, sniffed angrily and stamped his hoof in token that he resented any interference with his family's breakfast.

"What's the matter with him?" asked Joan in a whisper.

"Maybe he scented human beings watching him," suggested Anne.

Tally shook his head, but in another moment the scouts learned what had caused his annoyance. He now sounded a warning to the cows, and they all lifted their heads instantly and sniffed as the buck had done.

"Dear me, I hope they won't run away," wished Ruth, and then she saw that they would not run—they would defend themselves.

From out the dark fringe of forest there now crept a number of lean hungry timber-wolves, looking like long grey shadows of the trees. So slowly and noiselessly did they move that only animals trained to defend themselves in the wilderness would have known an enemy was so close at hand.

As they moved, the four men silently lifted their rifles, and waited for the signal from Tally to shoot.

"Are those the wolves we heard last night?" asked Julie.

"Most likely, or some like them," returned Mr. Gilroy, in a whisper that only those next him could hear.

"Um! t'ree of 'em—get reward fur dem coyotes!" grinned Omney.

The caribou, warned in time by the bull, saw the skulking beasts creeping, creeping like the shadows towards them, and they instantly formed their defence, as they always do in case of extreme danger when it is wiser to fight than to fly.

With their hind legs closed together like the center of a wheel, and their heads presenting antlers pointing towards the enemy like bayonets on the defence line in a battle, the herd stood perfectly still and waited.

"Wonderful sight!" breathed Mrs. Vernon.

"Oh, for that camera! It is in the duffel-bag," sighed Julie.

But the scene now grew too exciting for any scout to yearn over forgotten kodaks, for the wolves were almost near enough to begin their raid. The four rifles still pointed directly at them, but the signal was not yet forthcoming. Tally knew when to fire.

Just as the foremost wolf rose on his hind legs to hurl himself at the caribou nearest him, and the bull bellowed madly and wheeled to attack, Tally signaled. Four spurts of blue and four streaks of red—and three timber wolves rolled over dead!

At the sound of those dire sounds which the bull understood to be as deadly as a wolf, he lifted his snout high in the air, called hastily to his herd, and the wheel broke—the caribou trotted away swiftly and disappeared in the forest.

"That certainly was a sight worth seeing," sighed the Captain. "But I must hang that camera about my neck, day in and day out, or I shall miss the best pictures every time."

At breakfast that morning Mr. Gilroy said, "I had planned to cross the Continental Divide at Milner's Pass, because of the beauties of the Fall River Road, but this unexpected slide down from Flat Top yesterday, disarranged all these plans. What shall we do about it?"

"What was your next point of interest, had we gone over the pass as you had planned?" asked Mrs. Vernon.

"Well, you see, I thought we would land somewhere near Beaver Creek on the western slope of the Divide. I know a number of ranchers living about that section, and I thought the scouts might enjoy spending a week or so on these ranches."

"If it's all the same to you, Gilly, we'd rather enjoy the wildlife of the Rockies instead of ranching," ventured Julie.

"Oh, it's all the same. In fact, I'd rather not use any time on the ranches while I still have many interesting moraines to explore," said he.

"Then we'll plan a new route. What would you do next?" said the Captain.

"We are near the Meadow Fork of Grand River, I think, and we can follow that to reach Grand Lake. Then we can trail from there, along the North Fork of the Grand, until we reach Hot Sulphur Springs. After a visit to the Springs, we can go down Goré Canyon, cross the Goré Range, and thus reach Steamboat Springs."

"All right, let's do as you just said," remarked Mr. Vernon.

"Tally give up Devil-Bear and timber wolves at Spring," now said Tally.

"All right, Tally, but don't you think the girls ought to share in the reward for the wolves? We helped shoot them," said Mr. Gilroy.

"Um, sure! Scout git Devil-Bear money, too!" said Tally, amazed that any one should have thought otherwise.

"How so?" demanded Julie.

"Tally 'gree to guide, hunt, fish, help Mees'r Gilloy an' scout all way frough summer. Devil-Bear kill in hunt, but Tally paid for time," explained the Indian, thus refuting the reputation many white men give the Indian, that he will take advantage of other races every chance he gets.

"Oh, no, Tally! We wouldn't think of such a division!" exclaimed the Captain. "Give us the pelts and you take the reward."

As this suggestion was seconded by the others, Tally and Omney grinned joyously, for it was a windfall they had not looked for.

Further along the trail, Tally turned off to stop at a ranch-house and lay in a supply of flour and what other edibles the ranch-owner would sell him. Then they continued over the mountains.

Had the scouts come suddenly upon the Continental Divide they would have been speechless with the grandeur of it, but they had been riding past and over many peaks, canoeing down marvelous waterways, and had climbed all the ranges that led to the Divide, so that they scarcely realized that they were crossing the stupendous elevation until they heard Tally speak.

"Mos' over now, foothills all way to Sulphur Springs."

As they rode on, looking for Meadow Fork, along which Mr. Gilroy wished to trail, many questions were asked by the scouts and answered by the Indians.

Ruth then said, "I've heard a lot about Hot Sulphur Springs, Gilly, but what thrilling sight shall we find there?"

"Its name might lead you to believe you would see the apparition who is said to have charge of all sulphur worlds," said Julie, giggling.

"Also you will have an opportunity to taste the nastiest drinking water he—Julie's friend—ever sent bubbling forth," added Mr. Gilroy, quickly.

"That friend and I had a falling out and now we are not on speaking terms!" retorted Julie, and the others laughed.

"Why stop there, then? Let's go on to Goré's Canyon,—that sounds awfully thrilling," remarked Joan.

"Is it named Gory, Gilly, because so many Red Men scalped the early settlers out here?" asked Betty.

"Oh, no," laughed Mr. Gilroy. "It is named after an Irish nobleman, Sir George Goré, who discovered the canyon while he and a party of friends were hunting big game in the Rockies many years ago, before folks went over the Divide. In those days it was considered a marvelous feat to go into the Rockies."

"If every one can have a mountain named after them, why can't I have one called 'Juliet's Peak'?" demanded the irrepressible scout.

"You can, if you like. That is the easiest part of all, but how will other tourists know that that particular peak is named for *you*?" laughed Mr. Gilroy.

"You'd have to advertise the fact by some wild adventure, or great patriotic deed," added Mr. Vernon.

"Oh, I can advertise, all right!" retorted Julie. "I'll take a great bucket of whitewash and a calcimine brush; then on every flat-faced rock along the trail, up one side and down the other, I'll slap a hand-painted sign on every one of them: 'This is Juliet's Peak,' and the finger in ghostly white will point to my peak."

Her ridiculous explanation caused every one to laugh, but when Jolt turned and opened his jaw wide to emit the grating sound "Hee—haw! Hee—haw!" the riders declared it was screamingly opportune of the mule.

Late in the afternoon, the second day from Flat Top, the scouts had their first battle with a rattlesnake. It is claimed that one never sees a rattler on the east slope of the Rockies,—why, it is not stated. But one certainly encounters many of them on the west side and on other ranges in Colorado.

They were jogging along comfortably when Julie's horse suddenly leaped aside and climbed a steep bank beside the trail. The other horses trembled, and instantly the warning rattle sounded. Tally hurried back and saw a huge reptile coiled at one side of the trail, half-hidden under a bush.

He jumped from the saddle and snapped a hickory stick from a young sapling nearby. Then he whipped the rattler over the back. He could not break its back as the bush fended the blows. But Omney and Tally could so tire the reptile with blows that kept its head swinging from side to side, that finally they might jump on it.

The scouts sat and watched this interesting fight, the rattler darting its forked tongue venomously at the sticks, and in so doing having to turn its head from one to the other. This defence kept it from uncoiling and gliding away. Neither could it spring from the coil to strike while its head was so busy.

At last it showed signs of weariness, and once, when it momentarily forgot to strike at Tally's whip but struck twice in succession at the stick Omney wielded, the former took instant advantage of it, and in another moment his heel was planted upon the flat head.

Then the guides dragged the sinuous reptile out and measured it. It was fully five feet long, from head to tip of tail where ten rattles were attached. Tally removed these, and with a bow presented them to the Captain,—an honor shown all Tenderfeet in the Rockies, if a rattler is encountered by the natives.

"Him make fine money book, er belt," suggested Omney, when the scouts shuddered at the diamond-backed rattler.

"Oh, yes, we must send the skin home to be cured and made into souvenirs, girls!" exclaimed Mr. Gilroy.

In vain did the riders look for other rattlers after that, for every one wanted every skin that could be gotten for souvenirs.

Mr. Gilroy rode along, watching for the familiar landmarks that would tell him he had found Meadow Fork, but he finally admitted that he must have taken the wrong turn back by the ranch.

They rode past lovely streams and camped beside a most enchanting lake, then on, alongside a fine river, but Mr. Gilroy did not find his Meadow Fork or Grand Lake.

Finally, from the summit of one of the lower peaks on the western slope of the Rockies, the scouts saw a valley spread out before them, and concentrated in one spot of this valley were numerous dots, that were dwelling-houses, together with several large ones, that denoted they were hotels.

Mr. Gilroy rubbed his eyes, then stared. "Now, if I did not know better, I'd swear that that was Sulphur Springs."

"'Tis Sp'ings," chuckled Tally.

"But, Tally, it can't be! We haven't found Meadow Fork or Grand River, yet! Have we trailed along some other way?" wondered Mr. Gilroy.

The town proved to be the Springs, and there Mr. Gilroy learned that he had been riding along Meadow Fork, had camped at Grand Lake, and then followed Grand River, without knowing it. This error in judgment gave the scouts a never-ending chance for teasing him, thereafter.

That night the horses, as well as their riders, were glad to stretch out upon comfortable town-made beds, and in the morning the breakfast was already provided for all, instead of their having to first gather it.

The first thing the guides did after breakfast was to cash in their reward for Devil-Bear. The skin proved their claim, and word instantly circulated that two Indians had killed the menace of the ranches. The scouts received the reward for the tongues of the timber-wolves which Tally had brought into town, and thus the scouting party soon found fame camping on their doorstep. The local papers made much of them, and the girls took a keen delight in mailing home copies of the papers containing the account of their exploits.

CHAPTER THIRTEEN
A FOREST FIRE

"Now, friends, let us get away as soon as possible, or the guides may spend all their reward money on firewater, and be unable to start for a week," suggested Mr. Gilroy, confidentially, to the scouts.

"Why don't you take the money and deposit it for them in a bank?" asked Julie.

"I offered to keep it for them, but they were not overanxious to part with the cash. I know the boys too well to dream that they can withstand temptations of a town when they have such easy money to burn."

So the riders planned to leave immediately, starting away soon after the midday meal.

"I'm not sorry to leave the Springs with its ailing visitors behind," remarked Joan, as they got back into the saddles.

"Thank goodness we are not rheumatic, or gone to pieces, to have to come here to be mended again," declared Julie.

"I should think the horrid water would kill them, instead of curing," added Ruth, making a wry face at the remembrance of her taste of the waters.

"It isn't the water that cures, remember," said Mr. Gilroy, "it is the people's faith in it. And some folks believe that the more disagreeable a cure tastes, the better it will act."

From Hot Sulphur Springs the party rode through Goré Canyon, and then over the Goré Range, as Mr. Gilroy had planned. The climb up the latter mountains was one of the thrilling experiences of the trip.

Following Tally through an unbroken wilderness, they unexpectedly came upon an old lumber-road. Along this they trailed until it ended in a natural clearing of over a thousand acres. The park was surrounded by dense forests with apparently no trail leading from it.

"Here we are, boys! In, all right, but no way out," called Mr. Vernon, smiling at the perplexed looks of the riders.

"That means that every one has to hunt for a blaze of some kind," returned Mrs. Vernon.

"The blazes are here, all right, but the trail is such an old one that the young timber has, likely, grown up and hidden the old pines which carry the signs," added Mr. Gilroy.

Thereupon, every scout began to thrash through bushes and between young trees, hunting for the much-desired blaze. It was Betty's luck to find it, although she really wasn't looking as anxiously for it as were the other scouts.

She saw a queer scar on an old pine before her when she broke through some brush, and she was studying its strange formation when Tally came up behind her. He recognized the blaze and laughed.

"Betty find him! Come see!" shouted he.

The others galloped across the park and stared at the deeply scarred pine, while Tally read its meaning to them.

"It must have been blazed in the days of the First People," said Julie.

But little attention was paid her remark, as every one was eager to go on. Tally broke a way through the jungle of bush and young timber, and finally they all came out to the silent woods again.

They rode through twilight forests of gigantic red-spruce trees, measuring from three to six feet in diameter and towering over a hundred feet in height. The ground under these was carpeted with pine needles, which lay, year after year, until no sound echoed from the hoofbeats upon them.

Looking in any direction, the scouts could see only dense forests, with not a crevice in their vaulted roofs of green where the sun might filter through. These pines seemed to waft down virgin incense upon the heads of the riders, who fully appreciated the still beauty of the place, and the velvety corridors they went along.

Then the trail became steeper, and the trees grew smaller, allowing great splashes of sunshine to bask here and there upon the passive treetrunks, or to sprawl out upon the thick pine needles that covered the ground.

After riding for several hours, the scouts left the pine forest behind, and rode out upon a faint trail that ran through aspen brakes. Now and then they came to parks where the trail lost itself, and every one had to seek for it again.

A great deal of time was lost in each park they came to, over thus finding the trail, as so many misleading ones were made in the thick buffalo grass by wild animals that came to graze there. The only thing Tally relied upon for the right way was by finding a blaze upon an old tree nearby.

During the climb, the horses often came upon sudden precipitous descents that had to be zigzagged down through loose stone and débris, then up again on the other side. When the riders reached the highest altitude of the Goré Range and looked about, they found themselves among sheer cliffs, that obstructed any distant views.

"Feels like lunchtime to me," ventured Anne.

"I should think you'd say dinnertime—that's the way it feels to me," laughed Julie.

"I was afraid to say that, because I am always credited,—unjustly of course,—with being the gourmand of the Troop," retorted Anne.

Tally now led along a trail that ran through a small park, that lay between two towering cliffs which shut off all sight of anything on either side of them. Along the bottom of this ravine-like park a clear stream of water gurgled noisily.

"Shall we camp here for luncheon?" asked the Captain, seeing the sweet green grass and cooling stream.

"Oh, no, Verny! Let's find some woods to stop in. It's not very inviting to feel shut in so far down," returned Julie.

So they rode on, the horses picking their careful way over stones and roots, and their riders having to pay strict attention to the trail.

The trail wound about upthrusts of rock, where other streams ran to fall down the sides of the ravine, causing it to widen as it needed more space to carry the added waters. And at last, the scouts could see, in the distance, that the cliffs ahead ended and the stream also passed from view.

"Where the cliffs end will be a dandy spot for camp. We shall be able to sit and gaze over the park that most likely is to be found there," suggested Joan, eagerly.

"If you don't camp somewhere soon, you'll find me ended there!" sighed Anne, comically.

Before they reached this "end" however, the Captain held up a hand for silence, as she said, "That's a queer sound I hear!"

The others reined in their horses and listened. They then heard it, also. Mr. Vernon said, "Sounds like thunder, I think."

"No, it sounds more like a stampede of cattle on a ranch. If you've ever heard the hoofbeats of a herd of steer, you'd know that this is like it," came from Mr. Gilroy.

Tally grinned at both men. "Him waterfall!"

"Waterfall! All that volume of sound?" asked Mr. Gilroy, skeptically.

"Him *big waterfall*," repeated Tally.

"Let's hurry to find it, then!" declared Julie, urging her horse forward and gaining the corner of the cliff at the end of the ravine, ahead of her companions.

The crags completely hid all that might be beyond them; but as the riders went along, the volume of sound increased until the roaring of water convinced every one that the Indian must be right in his surmise. Then they passed around the obstructing crag, and sat spellbound at the panorama spread out before them.

The first glimpse of this tremendous waterfall was that of tawny green water bounding headlong over the precipice. Its dynamic vehemence had cleft a fearful way through the crags on either side of it, and adown its course one could see black hulks of rock that projected out from the swirling flood. The roar and thunder of this tremendous stream prevented any one from hearing other sounds.

The group of riders sat enthralled by the sight, then they next permitted their eyes to wander beyond the immediate falls to the magnificent view spread out in such space below and beyond. In the far distance the snow-capped peaks lay, one behind the other, until they were lost to sight in the drifting clouds on the horizon. But, as if loath to merge so quickly with the clouds, here and there one or more peaks would appear with their sharp points above the mist, and there reflect the glory of the shining sun.

From the far horizon and its peaks, the eyes now dropped gradually from one height to the next lower down, until they rested upon a valley that lay fully fifteen hundred feet below the crags where the scouts stood. The panorama was so vast in extent and so impressive in its sense of infinitude, that the spectators scarcely drew their breath.

The whole scene shimmered through the soft clouds that hung above the waterfalls and made it look like the reflections in a soap-bubble, with iridescent colors shining on the sphere. So ethereal appeared the picture that it seemed as if a slight vibration would surely shatter the bubble. This grand painting had existed here for centuries before the coming of the scouts to admire it, and there it promised to remain intact for centuries more after mortals should pass from the earth.

Here and there across this valley a ribbon of water wound a silent course away out of sight. From the great falls a mighty river flowed for miles until that, too, appeared like a silver ribbon, tying the land fancifully in its loops.

The silence was broken at last by Anne. "Can we find a better place for dinner than this grand cliff?"

The tension broke with a snap, and the others glared at the perplexed scout. Finally Julie cried, scornfully, "Can you find anything in that scene besides patches where food is grown?"

Good-natured Anne laughed, and shrugged her shoulders. "I think it is as beautiful as the Great Spirit ever made, but unfortunately I am not yet entirely spiritual. I find I must eat a bite now and then, to enable me to enjoy these pictures."

Her excuse for the interruption made every one laugh, and Mrs. Vernon then added, "I think Anne's suggestion very good,—to camp here and have dinner."

"Let Hominy lead the horses back to the grassy ravine to graze, while Tally cooks dinner," added Mr. Vernon.

So Omney rode back, leading the rest of the horses and the two pack-mules. Tally soon had the dinner cooking, but there was no chance of catching fish in that swift water, so they were satisfied that day with pork and beans, bread and jam for dinner.

After descending the last rampart of the Goré Range, the scouts heard Tally speak confidently of the locality they were in, but Mr. Gilroy seemed to differ with the guide.

"Me think us mos' here," insisted the Indian.

"Maybe you're right! I was mistaken before, so I'll give in," laughed Mr. Gilroy.

"What is it, Gilly?" asked some of the scouts.

"Tally says we are nearly at Steamboat Springs, and I say we are not. Now we will see who is right!"

They had not gone much farther along the trail, however, before the scouts discovered strawberries! Great luscious wild berries they were, and growing profusely everywhere in the grass.

"I guess Tally was right," admitted Mr. Gilroy. "We're in the wonderful strawberry belt that is so famous about Steamboat Springs."

Colorado strawberries are as famous, throughout the West, as the Rockyford melons are in the East; so the scouts made the most of their opportunity to eat the delicious berries while they were at the Springs. They visited the plants where berries are packed and shipped, and also visited a factory where jams were prepared.

This progressive little town, although so young, compared favorably with the larger cities of the East. It was equipped with electric light, telephones, paved streets, first-class public service, and other modern welfare improvements.

The evening after the scouts had visited the packing-houses that shipped strawberries to the markets, Mr. Gilroy sat studying a large map. Julie kept silent for a long time (for her) and finally spoke.

"What's the map for? Any change in plans?"

"I was figuring out whether or not we might possibly have time to go on a tangent trip, and take in Yellowstone Park, as long as we are so near Wyoming," he returned.

"Oh, fine! Do let's do that, Verny!" cried several of the girls.

"But that means an extended trip, Mr. Gilroy, and I do not see how we are going to finish all you have planned and still get back to Denver in time to take these girls back to school in September," remonstrated Mrs. Vernon.

An argument instantly followed, in which the scouts sided with Mr. Gilroy, arguing that time was no consideration when such wonderful sights as the geysers of the Yellowstone could be seen. Mrs. Vernon was firm, however, in her protest that school came before all such other considerations. Mr. Vernon also added his weighty decision by saying that he had to be back in New York City the first week in September, without fail.

"Then we will have to retrace our trail across the Rockies and travel slowly southward on the west side of the mountains," was Mr. Gilroy's reluctant rejoinder.

"Does that mean we can't go any farther than Steamboat Springs?" asked Julie, querulously.

"We might go on to Craig, and visit Cedar Mountain from the peak of which we can look over into Wyoming. That seems to be as near to it as we will come this summer," laughed Mr. Gilroy.

Julie pouted, and the other scouts sat and waited for developments. Mr. Vernon thought for a time, then turned to his friend with a suggestion.

"You wanted to cross the Divide at Milner's Pass because of the scenic beauty of the Fall River Road; now, why not cross it in going back to the eastern slope of the Rockies, and thence turn south?"

"I had thought of doing that, but the point at issue now seems Wyoming 'to be or not to be?'"

"That was just settled, as far as Uncle and I are concerned," added Mrs. Vernon, hastily. "It's 'not to be' because I swore solemnly that these girls would be home before Labor Day if they were permitted to take this trip. So home we go in time to begin school the first day of the Fall term."

"Dear me! It looks as if Verny had the wire-pulling this time!" sighed Joan, in such a tone that every one laughed.

"And of course where *she goes*, I have to follow!" said Ruth.

"Yes, sort of a 'Ruth and Naomi' proposition," retorted Julie.

This decision reached, without further resistance from the scouts, they retired for the night with the plan agreed upon to leave Steamboat Springs in the morning and start for the Park Range of the Divide.

The packs had been well filled for the new venture in the mountains, and having breakfasted royally early in the morning, the tourists started out on the trail. The horses had had such a good rest and the mules were so frisky again, that the line of riders made splendid time from Steamboat Springs to the hills.

They had climbed up one mountain and down the other side, then the next one, and then another, until Tally called a halt for something to eat. It was long past noon, and the horses were hungry, too. They were very near the summit of one of the lower ranges of mountains, and Mr. Gilroy suggested that they go on to the top and there rest and eat.

"And look out for a stream of water which is palatable for use," added Mr. Vernon.

As they rode to the summit of the mountain, the scouts conversed with Mr. Gilroy on various matters. But the thing that seemed to impress them most, was the fact that here they were back in the same mountains, and yet every day added new scenes and delights to the tour.

"It really doesn't seem as if we had ever been in one of these mountains before, because every step brings out new wonders," remarked Mrs. Vernon, as they all neared the top of the peak they had been ascending.

The sound of falling water now attracted Tally's attention, and he broke into the heavy undergrowth to locate the stream. This done, he came back and reported that he had found a fine place for the dinner.

They all dismounted at the spot, and the two men started downstream to fish, while the guides assigned various tasks to the different members of the party. Then, when the scouts had finished their work and the men were not yet back from fishing, they climbed to a crag of rock whence they expected to have a fine view.

"Well, did you ever!" exclaimed Ruth, the first to reach the top of the crag.

"What a queer fog for a mountainside!" was Julie's reply.

The other scouts now crowded up to see what caused these remarks, and as they gazed down upon a thick mantle of yellow, one of the girls called to Mrs. Vernon. She hastily climbed up beside them and looked as perplexed as her charges.

"Tally," called she, turning to beckon the Indian, "see if this is smoke, will you?"

"Him smoke!" affirmed Tally, the moment he saw the blanket beneath them.

"What! A fire in the forest?" cried several of the girls.

"Then we can't go through, can we?" asked Julie.

"Mebbe. Us wait and see," returned Tally. "But scout get camera ready *dis* time. Fine picksher pooty soon when an'mals run f'om fire."

"Verny, get the camera! Hurry up!" exclaimed the scouts, while Tally returned to his cooking.

His indifference to the fire that enveloped the forest tended to allay any fears they might have had. So they sat and watched the consuming flames as they swept across the forest and everywhere destroyed the fine timber. Unfortunately, the fire started at the base of the mountain so it quickly spread upward; had it begun at the top it would have burned itself out slowly for lack of fuel above where the draught always blows it.

Joan now leaned forward, and cried, "Look, quick!"

The scouts turned to gaze in the direction she pointed, and saw a number of beavers crossing a small park in order to reach a stream that flowed through the clearing. Immediately after the colony of beavers came a few deer, stopping now and then to turn and stare wonderingly at the heat that caused them such discomfort.

Then, to the amazement of the scouts, a large bear followed upon the heels of the deer, but he had no thought now of making a meal of venison. He seemed anxious only to reach a place where smoke and fire would not annoy him. Now and then the girls saw him stop, return a few paces and sound a queer growl. Then they saw the cause of this action.

A fat little cub finally ran out from the thick blanket of smoke, and hurried after its mother. When it came up to the old bear, it jumped about gleefully, never dreaming of the danger they were fleeing from. But the she-bear evidently thought this was no time for unseemly play, and gave the cub a smart cuff over the ear. The little fellow rolled over with the force of the slap, but then ran along beside his mother in meek submission to authority.

Tally now joined them again on the crag, and when the scouts had told of the bear, Ruth added, "But there are no birds escaping, Tally."

"Dem gone long go. Fire drive dem firs'."

"I'm glad of that, but just think of all the fledglings that *can't* fly and escape," said Betty.

"Let's think of something pleasanter," retorted Julie.

"Yes, let's think of dinner that Tally says is waiting," added Anne, laughingly.

As they sat down to dine, the scouts saw Omney sitting up on their former post of observation. As they wanted to ride on as soon as possible, one of the scouts asked why the guide didn't eat his dinner, too.

"Him watch if fire jump. Him kin eat dere as here."

"The fire is burning the other way, Tally," said Julie.

"Mebbe him jump back, if wind change. So Omney watch."

"If it blows this way, what must we do?" asked the Captain.

"Ride back trail us come. An' ride fas', too."

But the fire kept on burning its way in the direction it began to go, and after a long rest on the crags to permit the pall of smoke to be blown away, the guides led the way down the slope. All the down-timber had been burned to ash which was still hot in spots. So the horses picked their way between these heaps. Every vestige of brush, all vegetation, and living creatures were gone. Charred tree trunks showed where the flames had licked up the bark to get at the pine branches overhead, and there, high above the heads of the riders, the fire still raged through the resinous tops.

"It's a Sodom and Gomorrah for desolation, isn't it?" said Julie.

In all the fire-swept district the scouts saw not one charred body of animals that live in the woods. A coyote lay at the edge of the area, dead from the blow of an animal with sharp claws, but that had happened after the fire. Julie thought the bear probably did it because the horrid little coyote tried to get a bite of fat little cub.

"But see all the poor, poor trees," sighed Betty.

"Yes, these fires destroy more timber than all other forces put together," returned Mr. Gilroy. "Because of the resinous matter in pine or spruce, they burn quicker and make a hotter fire than other trees. But fortunately for future forests, the flames never can reach the roots and seedlings buried under ground, so these shortly sprout up and start new timber.

"It is not often that a fire sweeps over the same area again for centuries, unless some fool tenderfoot leaves a campfire burning, or shakes the hot ashes from a pipe."

They all rode forward as quickly as possible, for night was coming on apace, and every one was anxious to get out of the burnt district before dark. So they pitched camp as soon as they got beyond the fire line.

That night, flares like torches shot up from many of the standing trees on the hillside, and they continued burning for several days after the under fire had passed along. The light from these treetops cast weird shadows upon the camp.

"I never want to see another forest-fire," declared Joan, as she turned her face away from these flickering glares.

"None of us do, but as long as there *was* a fire, we are glad to have seen it," replied Julie.

"And I'm glad it was a *little* one," added the Captain.

"You wouldn't say that was a little fire, would you?" asked several of the scouts.

"Tally said it was not over a mile frontage, and that, he says, is a small one. If we saw a fire that stretched for miles along a forest ridge and kept on burning for days and days,—that, he claims, would be a big fire!"

All through that night blood-curdling cries came from the devastated district. The howls of panthers, growls of the bears, cries of coyotes, and yelps of timber-wolves, kept the campers awake. In the morning, Tally started early to seek the cause of such a clamor in the night.

"Dat ole dead coyote! Him mak all dat trubble," laughed the guide, upon his return to camp. "Dem starvin' an'mals all wand'da eat him, so dey fight and fight, but ole grizzle fight bes' an' git him."

CHAPTER FOURTEEN
LOST IN THE BAD LANDS

The following day the guides led the way up and down the sides of mountains, sometimes the trail running beside steep cliffs that rose sheer above the tourists' heads, and again past ravines where rushing, tumbling waters silenced all other sounds.

About noon of the third day after leaving Steamboat Springs, they reached the steepest climb of that trip. As they were nearing the top of the peak, Tally's horse suddenly fell over on its side and kicked its heels wildly.

The guide managed to jump clear of the leather and wild kicks, but the other riders sat speechless with fear at what was going to be the result of this awful spectacle. Before any one had time to offer help, however, the horse Mr. Gilroy rode did the same. The scouts immediately started to dismount, for they feared what might happen if their animals rolled and plunged as the first two were doing.

"Are they having fits?" asked Julie, anxiously.

"No, the unusually steep climb and the altitude affects horses this way quite often," explained Mr. Gilroy.

"I wish they'd let the rider know before they flop that way," said Joan, "then we might jump clear of their hoofs."

"If one had time to warn others of what was about to happen unexpectedly, very few people would have accidents," laughed Mrs. Vernon.

In a few minutes the horses got upon their feet, shook themselves thoroughly, and then waited to proceed on the trail.

Another halfhour's climb and they all reached the top of the peak. After leaving the timber-line, the riders found the scrub bushes grew scraggier and shorter, and finally the top of the peak was left as bare and craggy as any volcanic formation. From the top of one of these crags, Tally peered across an expanse of what looked like a rolling sea, but it was grey instead of blue-green.

When Mr. Gilroy saw this sea of sand, he quickly adjusted his glasses and gazed silently for a long time.

"Well, Tally, what do you make it out to be?" asked he.

"Him Bad Land—but I not know him in our way," returned the guide, apologetically.

"That's what I think about him—very bad land," chuckled Mr. Vernon, shading his eyes with both hands and staring down at the desert.

"What does that mean, Uncle? Do we have to cross it?" asked Julie.

"Either cross it, or go back the way we climbed and try to go around it—that means several days wasted on back-trailing."

"I can just discern the tiny thread of a trail that winds a way across that desert to the other side. We can easily follow the track and do it in one afternoon," said Mr. Gilroy.

"You don't think we shall be running any risks, do you?" ventured Mrs. Vernon.

"None whatever. If we were down at the base of this peak, right now, you would see how simple a thing it is to ride across the sand. The only danger in these Colorado wastes is when a storm threatens. But the sky is as clear as can be, and the day is too far spent now, for the sun to start anything going."

"The only hazard we take in crossing the sand waste, is that darkness may overtake us before we reach the other side, and that might cause us to stray from the trail," suggested Mr. Vernon.

"With two good guides to lead us, we take no risk on that score," returned Mr. Gilroy.

"At least it will prove to be a novel trip—climbing mountains and riding over a desert of sand all in the same day," said Julie, eagerly willing to try the experience.

Luncheon was hastily disposed of, and Tally led them all down the steep trail of the mountainside for several hours. Then they reached the lodgepole pine, which is the only timber that can hold out against desert storms in bad weather and in winter.

"Before we begin this desert ride, do let's look for some water," begged Ruth. "I'm thirsty as a sandpiper."

"Quite appropriate, too, as long as we are going to be closely affiliated with the sand," giggled Joan.

Tally and the two men had gone on before, and had not heard Ruth's request, or they might have spared the scouts a great deal of unpleasantness. They had hoped to strike the trail they had seen across the desert, so they rode in different directions to locate it, and the captain and girls were left to amble slowly along until one or all of the men returned for them.

So it happened that Ruth and Joan wandered about in search of drinking-water, and shortly after they left the rest of the scouts, Mrs. Vernon heard Ruth call.

"Come here! We've found a lovely little spring!"

The girls quickly followed in the newly broken trail that was plainly seen, and reached the pool of water that was hidden by sagebushes and low lava-rock formation.

"I was so thirsty I just flattened myself out on the sand and filled up," laughed Ruth, sighing with repletion.

Every one, the Captain included, drank freely of the warm water, and Julie made a remark that it tasted brackish for such an active spring.

"Maybe that is due to the sand and sun," ventured Joan.

"While we are here, let's give the horses a good drink," suggested Anne.

"That's a good idea. Then they will be fresh for the trip across the sand," added Mrs. Vernon, starting back to get her horse and lead him to the spring.

But the horses refused to drink. They seemed thirsty enough, but every one of them backed away when the girls tried to make them bend their heads and drink.

"Why, isn't that funny? Did you ever see them act like this before?" asked Julie.

Just then Tally's voice was heard calling for them, and the scouts jumped back into the saddles and rode forward. When they explained about the animals refusing the water, Tally looked serious.

"Show me drink!" commanded he, hurrying his horse over to the spring where the girls had drank.

One taste of the water and he made a wry face.

"You say you tak him?" asked the guide anxiously.

"Yes, lots of it," replied Ruth.

"Him mos' bad as dem bad land. Dat alkali water."

"What do you mean, Tally?" anxiously asked several girls.

"Him mak mucha ache here," explained Tally, placing his hands over his stomach and bending low with an agonized expression.

But the damage was done and so the scouts had to make the best of the case. Consequently, it was not long before Ruth was tied into knots and hardly able to sit in the saddle. The others, according to the quantity they had taken, were griped also. This did not add anything to the pleasure of the ride across the hot dry sand. But as long as they had essayed to cross that day, they kept on going slowly, hoping that with each cramp the scouts would begin to recover from the effects of the water.

Tally and his friend had been so certain that they would reach the other side of the desert before dark, that no one felt the slightest apprehension on that score. But the slowness with which the scouts had to travel made it dubious whether the riders would gain the other side before night.

Here and there, scattered over the desert sand, were queer craggy formations of lava, as if some volcanic eruption had thrown the heaps of burnt-out lava broadcast, to rest for ages upon the sea of waste. There was a constant wind blowing across the desert, that carried the tiniest particles of sand with it, and these cut into faces and uncovered parts of the flesh of horses and riders. This stinging sand added no little to the misery of the suffering scouts.

The men and two guides felt very sorry for their companions, yet they had to keep on riding because it was necessary that they reach safety and shelter for that night. Thinking to divert their thoughts from their pain, Mr. Gilroy called attention to an unusually large crag of lava that stood up like a peak from the undulating sea of sand around it.

"Suppose you take a snapshot of that queer formation," suggested Mr. Vernon, eager to abet his friend's plan.

"You take it, Uncle—We have no need of pictures any more. This promises to be our last day on earth," moaned Julie, her face drawn in pain.

They were quite near to the crag when Tally leaned forward in his saddle and held a hand to his ear in the attitude of one listening intently. Then he jumped from the horse and placed his ear flat down on the sand.

"What is it, Tally?" asked Mr. Gilroy, anxiously.

"Him blowin' bad! Can Messer Gilloy see much wind thoo glass?" questioned the guide, hastily, pointing off to the left.

Mr. Gilroy adjusted the glasses and gazed in the direction Tally pointed. Even the suffering scouts watched his face with more anxiety than they had given to the cramps.

"I fear we are in for a sandstorm, girls. We must make for that friendly crag and cower behind its out-thrusts until the worst is over," quickly advised Mr. Gilroy, as soon as he had satisfied himself that that was what the approaching cloud meant.

The two Indians urged their horses forward, and soon all were crouching down behind the meagre shelter offered by the ragged lava points. The horses were so placed that their bodies formed a screen for the riders, and the blankets and packs were arranged on the exposed sides of the animals to protect their skins from the stinging sand.

The sound of the wind as the storm rushed towards them, was awesome, but when the full fury of the simoon came, the sand was drifted quickly all about the horses and refugees. The wind fairly shrieked, as it tried to tear away the blankets and start a stampede of the horses, but the Indians were able to calm the poor animals' fear.

The windstorm blew over as suddenly as it came, and the moment the going was safe, Tally led the horses from their drifts of sand and saddled them again. The riders crawled out, also, and shook themselves free of the clinging sand, then got back in their saddles, ready to ride onward.

The guides had not gone far, however, before they realized that the sandstorm had played greater havoc with the faint trail than with the riders. Such was the menace they now had to face: Night coming on apace, the scouts with cramps from alkali water, horses thirsty and sore from the beating of the simoon, and still an endless waste to cross, and no pathway to guide them.

"Oh, why did we ever come this way?" wailed Mrs. Vernon.

"We mos' over him," soothed Tally.

"Why, we've been riding for hours, and still there is nothing but sand to be seen," complained Julie.

"All same, us fin' end pooty soon," returned Omney.

They rode on without much conversation after that, as no one felt cheerful enough to talk. The sun had set beyond the rolling sea of sand, and yet no welcome sight of trees or dwellings could be seen before them. Nothing but sand, sand, sand!

After the sun had completely disappeared, a chill crept into the air and in ten minutes time every one was shivering with cold. Tally spoke in undertones to Mr. Gilroy, and he in turn said to his companions, "Let every one get the guide-rope out and tie it to the saddle in front of you."

"Why," called Joan.

"Anything left in Pandora's box for us poor creatures?" asked Julie sorrowfully.

"Tally thinks one of us might stray, if the darkness overtakes us as suddenly as it falls on these deserts sometimes," said Mr. Gilroy.

Before every one was hitched securely to the horse in front, so that a long line of riders traveled in file, a soughing wind could be heard coming from the north.

"Now, what can that be? More trouble?" demanded Mrs. Vernon.

"We hope not, but Tally says that quite often, after a hot sandstorm, it returns with sleet and hail; so we'd better be ready in case this chill portends such a comeback," explained Mr. Gilroy.

"What a fate! To drink poison, then fight a simoon, and at last to die in a desert blizzard!" cried Julie frantically trying to sit upright and defy the fates.

"Such is Rocky Mountain weather," Mr. Gilroy laughed gaily, as if he must inspire his friends with his bravado.

The oncoming blizzard had darkened the sky even before its time, but Tally kept bravely on, encouraging the horses with *coos* and Indian words, until even the riders felt the spirit he manifested and felt braver to face what was impending.

Just before the sleet began to drive into their faces enough to blind them and shut out everything not two feet ahead, Mr. Gilroy shouted out cheerfully, "Ha! I see a light twinkling out ahead! We've reached a house, anyway!"

"Where? where?" asked a chorus of voices.

Then most of them discerned the faint little beacon, and urged their weary horses to renewed effort, and the animals seemed to understand that their work was almost done for that day, and actually moved faster.

But the blizzard struck before they could reach the refuge, coating everything with ice and cutting deep into tender hands and faces. The horses were soon stiff with the cold, and it took all of the riders' energy, even so close to a promising haven, to keep the beasts moving.

Finally Tally shouted wildly, "Light ahead! Light here!"

And at the same time his horse stumbled down a steep grade into a rushing little brook. Omney saw the danger before his horse reached the bank, and warned all the others behind him. They crossed the water safely, and after scrambling up the steep bank on the other side, they found themselves in a barnyard.

They made such a noise at this discovery, that a man hurried from one of the low, long buildings with a lantern.

"Oh, welcome sight!" sighed Mrs. Vernon, ready to faint with joy and relief.

During a momentary lull in the wind and sleet, they all rode up to the long, low ranch house, and shouted to the owners to help them. Soon every one was thawing before a roaring fire; and the poor horses were in the stable, enjoying food and rest.

CHAPTER FIFTEEN
BACK-TRAILING TO DENVER

The ill effects of the alkali water passed off in a few hours, and the scouts felt able to continue the ride in the morning. The sun was shining so brightly that no one would have dared say there had been a fearful storm the night before. As they all sat about the rough table for breakfast, the host explained to Mr. Gilroy how the guides missed the right trail on the mountains, and he sketched for them a rude map to help them find the point where the Medicine Bow Mountains and Frontal Range met in the Continental Divide.

When the horses were brought to the door, and all were ready to start on the ride again, Mr. Vernon insisted upon the good mountain rancher taking a gift for his hospitality, although the latter demurred for sometime before he was prevailed upon to take the recompense.

That day Tally led his party along the well-defined trail he had missed the day before, and by sundown they were nearing the wonderful altitude and mountaintops of the Frontal Range.

At night they camped in one of the wildest spots of the mountains, where the extensive view was as imposing as any to be found in Colorado. Tally had, with true Indian instinct, found a small lake of purest cold water, where they could pitch camp. A wild animal trail circuited this lake, and while the guides prepared the supper, the Captain suggested a ride around the sheet of clear water.

The scene was splendidly wild, and isolation hung like a curtain over everything down below in the valley, that was seen through the forest trees whenever the scouts climbed a prominence. Mystic sounds chirruped at them as they rode slowly along the narrow path, lending enchantment to the beauty of the place.

The fast-fading rays of purple and rose that sped in the wake of the setting sun, cast ever-changing gleams of color across the placid lake. As the twilight advanced, the silence of the forest was felt, and only now and then came a wildwood sound to startle the scouts.

As they followed the trail that skirted the lake, they came to a rippling stream that had to be forded. Just as Julie, always in advance, guided her horse down the steep bank, a crackling of dry twigs on the other side caused the horse to stop suddenly.

"O girls! Look! Look!" whispered Julie, tensely.

There stood a fawn as if cut from stone, with ears erect and nose sniffing at the strange creatures seen so near at hand. Even as the scouts gazed admiringly, the graceful thing flaunted its short tail and, with the stamping of a hoof to protest against this interruption of her drink, disappeared, without a sound of its going.

They crossed the stream and were keeping on the trail that ran along the shore, when from overhead, a loon shrilled a warning to its mate across the lake that there was a strange horde of life passing under her tree! But the male loon sent back his wild laughter at such unbased fears of his wife's. All these incidents impressed the scouts with a sense of their being one with the wild creatures, and they regretted the fact that they were nearing camp again.

At the point where Tally had made the night camp, the reeds and grasses hugged the shore of the lake, and now a faint mist upcurled from the water like a transparent veil. Gradually this veil spread inland and quietly enveloped all things on shore. The bright fire dispelled the mist about the camp, and as the hungry scouts sniffed the odors of a good supper, the beauties of Nature were temporarily forgotten.

While the scouts were adventuring around the lake, Mr. Gilroy and Mr. Vernon had cut hemlock bows for bedding, so that all was ready for the night before supper was served. After enjoying Tally's cooking to the utmost, the scouts sat down to listen to the various wild adventures of Omney and Talley. But one after another, they dozed before long, and Mr. Gilroy suggested they all retire for the night.

Talley knew not how long he had been sleeping when he was unaccountably aroused as if by a strange noise in camp. He sat up and listened, but all seemed quiet, so he soon was dozing again. The snapping of a twig, some distance away, however, made him open his eyes drowsily and wonder sleepily if the horses were securely hobbled.

He was too tired to keep awake long enough to get up and go in search of the animals. The thought of it, however, before he fell sound asleep caused him to dream fitfully all night.

He awoke very early and got up to reassure himself that all was well in camp. He could see no sign of any horse or mule, so he shook Omney, and the two ran in search of the strayed animals.

When the rest of the touring party woke up to find the sun shining into their eyes, no sign of guides or horses was seen. Mr. Gilroy began to prepare breakfast, and Mr. Vernon was sent to fish. The girls were each detailed on some work, and by the time the meal was ready, sounds of hoofs were heard along the trail.

"Dat Jolt, he makka all horse go way down trail. Omney an' me fin' dem miles down," explained Tally, with a vindictive look at the mule. As if he fully understood the Indian, Jolt sent back an answering gleam from his wicked eyes and kicked up his hind legs in derision.

Mr. Vernon had caught more than enough fish in the overstocked lake, and when the fried mush, bacon, and fresh fish, bread, and fragrant coffee were served, the appetites displayed were such as would drive a New York boarding-house keeper distracted.

That day the scouts rode in forests where stately aromatic pines sheltered countless wild creatures, that peered from their cloistered haunts with wonderment at the strangers. Birds of every description sang from low-swinging branches, and lesser notes from unseen insects in the bushes and grass added music to this orchestra that rendered the grandest symphony ever heard.

That evening while seated about the camp supper, Julie said, "There's one animal I've wanted to see in his natural haunts in the Rockies, and not one have we been able to glimpse."

"What's that?" asked Mr. Gilroy.

"The famous American buffalo of the plains," returned she.

"Ah, it is the Captain's fault that you girls were not able to see the bison at home," retorted Mr. Gilroy. "Had she consented to your going with me to Yellowstone Park, you could have watched the animals grazing and wandering over their own fields."

"Well, the buffalo will still be there next year, but the scouts cannot lose a month of school this fall just to go and watch the animals in Wyoming," said Mrs. Vernon.

"Of course, your word is law to us all, but it does seem a pity, as I said before, that being so near the geysers, we should not take advantage of it," remarked Mr. Gilroy.

The scouts expressed in their faces that they thought on this matter exactly as Mr. Gilroy did, but the Captain said, "If you continue to preach your mutinous ideas to my girls, I'll leave you out of my plans next summer when we take a trip."

"Wough! That threat will keep me quiet for all time!" laughed Mr. Gilroy, clapping a hand over his mouth to show his instant obedience.

Every one laughed, but Tally now joined the circle and asked for orders for the next day's ride. After talking over various trails and plans, they got up and prepared to retire for the night.

"Did any one hang up the saddles to-night?" asked Mr. Vernon, before he turned in to sleep.

"Tally, did you look after the leather?" asked Mr. Gilroy.

Tally turned to Omney, "Did him fix harness?"

"Me do it, all light," returned Omney, then he shuffled out of the circle of light cast by the fire and they heard him fumbling with heavy saddles and other trappings.

The glorious break of day in the mountains awoke every one, and soon the breakfast was under way. While the guides cooked, Mr. Vernon went for the horses. Mr. Gilroy decided to save time by taking down the harness from the trees where it was usually hung.

"Great Scout!" called he, summoning the Indians to the spot.

"What's the matter?" asked the scouts, anxiously running after the two guides.

"A rascally porcupine has been at our leather last night!" declared Mr. Gilroy, angrily showing the ravages made on the harnesses.

Tally glared at Omney, "Why for you do dat? Don' you know dem bad rats eat all up?"

Omney said nothing, but looked very penitent. Mr. Gilroy sighed as he began an inventory of the damage.

"Two sets of reins chawed to pieces; a throat latchet gone; three saddles with holes eaten through them, and two bridles cut to bits, all because of a little carelessness!"

"I fixa dem allight!" exclaimed Omney, eagerly.

"But that means a morning lost while you make repairs," replied Mrs. Vernon.

Then Omney stiffened his spine and lifted his head in a majestic fury at the porcupines. He glowered down the trail and shook his clenched fist vengefully at the imaginary depredator, saying in hissing voice, "Him one bad darn beas'!"

Every one laughed at his suppressed fury, and the tame exclamation he had just used, but the poor guide felt better again.

The harnesses were finally mended with rope and bits of wire from Tally's outfit kit, and by noon everything was in readiness for continuing the trip.

Toward the end of August, the tourists reached Estes Park again, and upon riding to Long's peak village, they replaced the mended harness with good sections, and then rode on to Loveland, where they proposed leaving the horses they had leased for the summer.

While Mr. Gilroy and Tally led the horses back to their owner, the Captain took the girls to the department store and soon they were busy trying on readymade dresses that they might start for Denver. Mrs. Vernon had strenuously vetoed their appearing in civilization again in the patched and faded scout uniforms that had stood such rough usage while camping in the mountains.

But the uniforms were carefully packed to take back home as souvenirs of that eventful summer.

When shop-made shoes were tried on the feet that had been free all summer from city footgear, and the scouts tried to walk on the stone pavements of Loveland, they winced with the pain of their toes in cramped quarters.

"Goodness, girls! Isn't it awful to have had such freedom all summer and then return to prison cells again for feet and body?" cried Julie, frowning.

"Yes, and it will be the same when we go to bed to-night, no more forest vastness for a chamber, no more pine for a roof, and no more singing of wild notes to lull us to sleep!" sighed Joan.

That evening Mr. Gilroy condoled with the scouts over the immediate future—school, orthodox clothing, and bandbox rooms to live in all winter.

"But there is always the hope of heaven before you," said Mr. Vernon, smiling at the circle of faces.

"What do you mean?" asked Julie.

"There is next summer again, you know, and if Gilroy is as good as his word, he will see that you are escorted to Arizona and New Mexico for a trip!"

"Remind me of it next spring, girls, and we'll see," laughed Mr. Gilroy, winking an eye at the Captain.

So with this ray of hope for a future outing, the girls were encouraged to start back East, and take up the irksome tasks of acquiring a necessary education in the humdrum daily lessons of school.